THE
STAR
KING

Jack Vance

A BERKLEY MEDALLION BOOK
published by
BERKLEY PUBLISHING CORPORATION

Chapter 1

"What a paradox, what a fearful reproach, when the distinction of a few hundred miles—nay, as many feet or even inches!—can transform heinous crime to simple unqualified circumstance!"

...Hm. Balder Bashin, in the Ecclesiarchic Nunciamento of Year 1000 at Foresse, on the planet Krokinole.

"Law cannot reach where enforcement will not follow."

...Popular aphorism.

Excerpts from "Smade of Smade's Planet," feature article in *Cosmopolis,* October, 1923:

Q: Do you ever get lonesome, Mr. Smade?

A: Not with three wives and eleven children.

Q: Whatever impelled you to settle here? A rather dismal world, on the whole, isn't it?

A: Beauty is in the eye of the beholder. I don't care to run a vacation resort.

Q: What kind of people patronize the tavern?

A: People who want quiet and a chance to rest. Occasionally a traveler from inside the Pale or an explorer.

Q: I've heard that some of your clientele is pretty rough. In fact—not to mince words—it's the general belief that Smade's Tavern is frequented by the most notorious pirates and freebooters of the Beyond.

A: I suppose they occasionally need rest too.

Q: Don't you have difficulty with these people? Maintaining order, so to speak?

A: No. They know my rules. I say, "Gentlemen, please desist. Your differences are your own; they are fugitive. The harmonious atmosphere of the tavern is mine and I intend it to be permanent."

Q: So then they desist?

A: Usually.
Q: And if not?
A: I pitch them into the sea.

* * * * * * *

Smade was a reticent man. His origins and early life were known only to himself. In the year 1479 he acquired a cargo of fine timber, which, for a whole set of obscure reasons, he took to a small stony world in the middle Beyond. And there, with the help of ten indentured artisans and as many slaves, he built Smade's Tavern.

The site was a long narrow shelf of heath between the Smade Mountains and Smade Ocean, precisely on the planet's equator. He built to a plan as old as construction itself, using stone for the walls, timber beams and plates of schist for the roof. Completed, the tavern clung to the landscape, as integral as an outcrop of rock: a long two-storied structure with a high gable, a double row of windows in front and rear, chimneys at either end venting smoke from fires of fossil moss. At the rear stood a group of cypress trees, their shape and foliage completely appropriate to the landscape.

Smade introduced other new features into the ecology: in a sheltered valley behind the tavern he planted fodder and garden truck; in another he kept a small herd of cattle and a flock of poultry. All did moderately well, but showed no disposition to overrun the planet.

Smade's dominion extended as far as he cared to claim—there was no other habitation on the planet—but he chose to assert control only over an area of perhaps three acres, within the bounds of a whitewashed stone fence. From occurrences beyond the fence Smade held aloof, unless he had reason to consider his own interests threatened—a contingency which had never arisen.

Smade's Planet was the single companion of Smade's Star, an undistinguished white dwarf in a relatively empty region of space. The native flora was sparse: lichen, moss, primitive vines and palodendron, pelagic algae which tinctured the sea black. The fauna was even simpler: white worms in the seabottom muck; a few gelatinous creatures which gathered and ingested the black algae in a ludicrously inept fashion; an assortment of simple protozoa. Smade's alterations of the planet's ecology could hardly, therefore, be considered detrimental.

6

Smade himself was tall, broad, and stout, with bone-white skin and jet-black hair. His antecedents, as has been mentioned, were vague, and he never had been heard to reminisce; the tavern, however, was managed with the utmost decorum. The three wives lived in harmony, the children were handsome and well-mannered, Smade himself was unfailingly polite. His rates were high, but his hospitality was generous, and he made no difficulties about collecting his bill. A sign hung above the bar: "Eat and drink without stint. He who can and does pay is a customer. He who cannot and does not pay is a guest of the establishment."

Smade's patrons were diverse: explorers, locaters, Jarnell technicians, private agents in search of lost men or stolen treasure, more rarely an IPCC representative—or "weasel," in the argot of the Beyond. Others were folk more dire, and these were of as many sorts as there were crimes to be named. Making a virtue of necessity, Smade presented the same face to all.

To Smade's Tavern in the July of 1524 came Kirth Gersen, representing himself as a locater. His boat was the standard model leased by the estate houses within the Oikumene, a thirty-foot cylinder equipped with no more than bare necessities: in the bow the monitor-autopilot duplex, a star-finder, chronometer, macroscope, and manual controls; midships the living quarters with air machine, organic reconverter, information bank, and storage; aft the energy block, the Jarnell intersplit, and further storage. The boat was as scarred and dented as any; Gersen's personal disguise was no more than well-worn clothes and natural taciturnity. Smade accepted him on his own terms.

"Will you stay awhile, Mr. Gersen?"

"Two or three days, perhaps. I have things to think over."

Smade nodded in profound understanding. "We're slack just now; just you and the Star King. You'll find all the quiet you need."

"I'll be pleased for that," said Gersen, which was quite true; his just-completed affairs had left him with a set of unresolved qualms. He turned away, then halted and looked back as Smade's words penetrated his consciousness. "There's a Star King here, at the tavern?"

"He has presented himself so."

"I've never seen a Star King. Not that I know of."

Smade nodded politely to indicate that the gossip had reached to the allowable limits of particularity. He indicated the tavern clock: "Our local time; better set your watch. Supper at seven o'clock, just half an hour."

Gersen climbed stone stairs to his room, an austere cubicle containing bed, chair and table. He looked through the window, along the verge of heath between mountain and ocean. Two space craft occupied the landing field: his own and another ship, larger and heavier, evidently the property of the Star King.

Gersen washed in a hall bathroom, then returned to the downstairs hall, where he dined on the produce of Smade's own gardens and herd. Two other guests made their appearance. The first was the Star King, who strode to the far end of the room in a flutter of rich garments: an individual with skin dyed jet black, eyes like ebony cabochons as black as his skin. He was taller than average height, and carried himself with consummate arrogance. Lusterless as charcoal, the skin dye blurred the contrast of his features, made his face a protean mask. His garments were dramatically fanciful: breeches of orange silk, a loose scarlet robe with white sash, a loose striped gray and black coif which hung rakishly down the right side of his head. Gersen inspected him with open curiosity. This was the first Star King he had observed as such, though popular belief had hundreds moving incognito through the worlds of man: cosmic mysteries since the first human visit to Lambda Grus.

The second of the guests apparently had just arrived: a thin middle-aged man of indefinite racial background. Gersen had seen many like him, miscellaneous uncategorized vagabonds of the Beyond. He had short coarse white hair, a sallow undyed skin, an air of diffident uncertainty. He ate without appetite, looking back and forth between Gersen and the Star King in furtive speculation, but it seemed as if presently his most searching glances were directed toward Gersen. Gersen tried to avoid the increasingly insistent gaze; the least of his desires was involvement in the affairs of a stranger.

After dinner, as Gersen sat watching the play of lightning over the ocean, the man sidled close, wincing and grimacing in sheer nervousness. He spoke in a voice which he tried to keep even, but which trembled nevertheless. "I assume that you are here from Brinktown?"

From childhood Gersen had concealed his emotions behind a careful, if somewhat saturnine, imperturbability; but the man's question, jangling upon his own alarms and ten-

8

sions, startled him. He paused before replying, gave a mild assent. "As a matter of fact, I am."

"I expected to see someone else. But no matter. I've decided that I can't fulfill my obligation. Your journey is pointless. That's all." He stood back, teeth showing in a humorless grin—obviously braced against an expected dire reaction.

Gersen smiled politely, shook his head. "You mistake me for some else."

The other peered down in disbelief. "But you are here from Brinktown?"

"What of that?"

The man made a forlorn gesture. "No matter. I expected —but no matter." After a moment he said, "I noticed your ship—model 9B. You're a locater, then."

"Correct."

The man refused to be discouraged by Gersen's terseness. "You're on your way out? Or in?"

"Out." Then, deciding that it was as well to circumstantiate his role, he added, "I cant' say that I've had luck."

The other man's tension suddenly gave way. His shoulders sagged. "I own to the same line of business. As to luck—" He heaved a forlorn sigh, and Gersen smelled Smade's home-distilled whiskey. "If it's bad, no doubt I have myself to blame."

Gersen's suspicion was not completely lulled. The man's voice was well-modulated, his accent educated—in itself indicating nothing. He might be precisely as he represented himself: a locater in some sort of trouble at Brinktown. Or he might be otherwise: a situation entailing a set of hairraising corollaries. Gersen would vastly have preferred the company of his own thoughts, but it was an act of elementary precaution to look more deeply into the matter. He drew a deep sigh and, feeling faintly sorry for himself, made a courteous, if wry, gesture.

"Do you care to join me?"

"Thank you." The man seated himself gratefully, and with a new air of bravado seemed to dismiss all of his worries and apprehensions. "My name is Teehalt, Lugo Teehalt. Will you drink?" Without waiting for assent he signaled one of Smade's young daughters, a girl of nine or ten, wearing a modest white blouse and long black skirt. "I'll use whiskey, lass, and serve this gentleman whatever he decides for himself."

Teehalt appeared to derive strength either from the drink

9

or from the prospect of conversation. His voice became firmer, his eyes clearer and brighter. "How long have you been out?"

"Four or five months," said Gersen, in his role of locater. "I've seen nothing but rock and mud and sulfur ... I don't know whether it's worth the toil."

Teehalt smiled, nodded slowly. "But still—isn't there always excitement? The star gleams and lights up its circlet of planets. And you ask yourself, will it be now? And time after time: the smoke and ammonia, the weird crystals, the winds of monoxide, the rains of acid. But you go on and on and on. Perhaps in the region ahead the elements coalesce into nobler forms. Of course it's the same slime and black trap and methane snow. And then suddenly: there it is. Utter beauty...."

Gersen sipped his whiskey without comment. Teehalt apparently was a gentleman, well-mannered and educated, sadly come down in the world.

Teehalt continued, half talking to himself. "Where the luck lies, that I don't know. I'm sure of nothing. Good luck looks to be bad luck, disappointment seems happier than success.... But then, bad luck I would never have recognized as good luck, and called it bad luck still, and who can confuse disappointment with success? Not I. So it's all one and life proceeds regardless."

Gersen began to relax. This sort of incoherence, at once engaging and suggestive of a deeper wisdom, could not be imagined among his enemies. Unless they hired a madman? Gersen made a cautious contribution: "Uncertainty hurts more than ignorance."

Teehalt inspected him with respect, as if the statement had been one of profound wisdom. "You can't believe that a man is the better for ignorance?"

"Cases vary," said Gersen, in as easy and light a manner as was natural to him. "It's clear that uncertainty breeds indecision, which is a dead halt. An ignorant man can act. As for right or wrong—each man to his own answer. There never has been a true consensus."

Teehalt smiled sadly. "You espouse a very popular roctrine, ethical pragmatism, which always turns out to be the doctrine of self-interest. Still, I understand you where you speak of uncertainty, for I am an uncertain man." He shook his thin, sharp-featured head. "I know I'm in a bad way, but why should I not? I've had a peculiar experience." He finished the whiskey, leaned forward to gaze into Ger-

10

sen's face. "You are perhaps more sensitive than first impression would suggest. Perhaps more agile. And possibly younger than you seem."

"I was born in 1490."

Teehalt made a sign which could mean anything, searched Gersen's face once more. "Can you understand me if I say that I have known overmuch beauty?"

"I probably could understand," said Gersen, "if you made yourself clear."

Teehalt blinked thoughtfully. "I will try." He considered. "As I have admitted to you, I am a locater. It is a poor trade—with apologies to you—for eventually it involves the degradation of beauty. Sometimes only to a small extent, which is what a person such as myself hopes for. Sometimes there is only small beauty to corrupt, and sometimes the beauty is incorruptible." He made a gesture of his hand toward the ocean. "The tavern harms nothing. The tavern allows the beauty of this terrible little planet to reveal itself." He leaned forward, licking his lips. The name Malagate is known to you? Attel Malagate?"

For a second time Gersen was startled; for a second time the reaction failed to reach his face. After another slight pause, he asked casually, "Malagate the Woe, so-called?"

"Yes. Malagate the Woe. You are acquainted with him?" And Lugo Teehalt peered at Gersen through eyes which had suddenly gone leaden, as if the mere act of naming the possibility had renewed his suspicion.

"Only by reputation," said Gersen, with a bleak twitch of a smile.

Teehalt leaned forward with great earnestness. "Whatever you may have heard, I assure you, it is flattery."

"But you don't know what I have heard."

"I doubt if you have heard the worst. But nevertheless, and the astounding paradox. . . ." Teehalt closed his eyes. "I am locating for Attel Malagate. He owns my ship. I have taken his money."

"It is a difficult position."

"When I found out—what could I do?" Teehalt threw up his hands in an excited extravagant gesture, reflecting either emotional turmoil or the effects of Smade's whiskey. "I have asked myself this, over and over. I did not make this choice. I had my ship and my money, not from an estate house, but from an institution of dignity. I did not think of myself as a common locater. I was Lugo Teehalt, a man of parts, who had been appointed to the post of Chief Explorer for the

11

institution, or some such folly—so I assured myself. But they sent me out in a 9B boat, and I could no longer delude myself. I was Lugo Teehalt, common locater."

"Where is your boat?" asked Gersen, idly curious. "There is only my own and the Star King's out on the landing field."

Teehalt pursed his lips in another onset of wariness. "I have good reason for caution." Teehalt glanced right and left. "Would it surprise you to learn that I expect to meet—" he hesitated, thought better of what he had planned to say, and sat silently a moment, looking into his empty glass. Gersen signaled, and young Araminta Smade brought whiskey on a white jade tray, upon which she herself had painted a red and blue floral border.

"But this is inconsequential," said Teehalt suddenly. "I bore you with my problems...."

"Not at all," said Gersen, quite truthfully. "The affairs of Attel Malagate interest me."

"I can understand this," said Teehalt after another pause. "He is a peculiar combination of qualities."

"From whom did you have your boat?" Gersen asked ingenuously.

Teehalt shook his head. "I will not say. For all I know you may be Malagate's man. I hope not, for your own sake."

"Why should I be Malagate's man?"

"Circumstances suggest as much. But circumstances only. And in fact I know that you are not. He would not send someone here whom I have not met."

"You have a rendezvous, then."

"One I don't care to keep. But—I don't know what else to do."

"Return to the Oikumene."

"What does Malagate care for that? He comes and goes as he pleases."

"Why should he concern himself with you? Locaters are twenty to the dozen."

"I am unique," said Teehalt. "I am a locater who has found a prize too precious to sell."

Gersen was impressed in spite of himself.

"It is a world too beautiful for degradation," said Teehalt. "An innocent world, full of light and air and color. To give this world to Malagate, for his palaces and whirligigs and casinos—it would be like giving a child to a squad of Sarcoy soldiers. Worse? Possibly worse."

"And Malagate knows of this?"

12

"It is my unfortunate habit to drink rashly and talk wildly."

"As you do now," suggested Gersen.

Teehalt smiled his wincing morose smile. "You could tell Malagate nothing he does not already know. The damage was done at Brinktown."

"Tell me more of this world. Is it inhabited?"

Teehalt smiled again, but made no answer. Gersen felt no resentment. Teehalt, beckoning to Araminta Smade, ordered Fraze, a heavy sour-sweet liquor reputed to include among its constituents a subtle hallucinizer. Gersen signified that he would drink no more.

Night had long settled over the planet. Lightning crashed back and forth; a sudden downpour began to drum on the roof.

Teehalt, lulled by the liquor, perhaps seeing visions among the flames, said, "You could never find this world. I am resolved that it shall not be violated."

"What of your contract?"

Teehalt made a contemptuous motion. "I would honor it for an ordinary world."

"The information is on the monitor filament," Gersen pointed out. "The property of your sponsor."

Teehalt was silent so long that Gersen wondered if he were awake. Finally Teehalt said, "I am afraid to die. Otherwise I would drop myself and boat and monitor and all into a star."

Gersen had no comment to make.

"I do not know what to do." Teehalt's voice became soft, as the drink soothed his brain, and showed him visions. "This is a remarkable world. Beautiful, yes. I wonder if the beauty does not conceal another quality which I can't fathom ... just as a woman's beauty camouflages her more abstract virtues. Or vices.... In any event the world is beautiful and serene beyond words. There are mountains washed by rain. Over the valleys float clouds as soft and bright as snow. The sky is a deep dark sapphire blue. The air is sweet and cool—so fresh that it seems a lens. There are flowers, though not very many. They grow in little clumps, so that to find them is like coming on a treasure. But there are many trees, and most magnificent are the great kings, with gray bark, which seem to have lived forever.

"You asked if the world were inhabited. I am forced to answer yes, though the creatures who live there are—strange. I call them dryads. I saw only a few hundred, and they

13

seem a race ages old. As old as the trees, as old as the mountains." Teehalt shut his eyes. "The day is twice the length of ours; the mornings are long and bright, the noons are quiet, the afternoons are golden—like honey. The dryads bathe in the river or stand in the dark forest...." Teehalt's voice dwindled; he appeared to be half asleep.

Gersen prompted him. "Dryads?"

Teehalt stirred, raised in his chair. "It's as good a name as any. They're at least half plant. I made no real examination; I dared not. Why? I don't know. I was there—oh, I suppose two or three weeks. This is what I saw...."

* * * * * * *

Teehalt landed the battered old 9B on a meadow beside a river. He waited while the analyzer made environmental tests, though a landscape so fair could not fail to be hospitable—or so thought Teehalt, who was scholar, poet, wastrel in equal parts. He was not wrong: the atmosphere proved salubrious; allergen-sensitive cultures tested negative; microorganisms of air and soil quickly died upon contact with the standard antibiotic with which Teehalt now dosed himself. There seemed no reason why he should not immediately go forth upon this world, and he did so.

On the turf in front of the ship Teehalt stood entranced. The air was clear and clean and fresh, like the air of a spring dawn, and utterly silent, as if just after a bird call.

Teehalt wandered up the valley. Stopping to admire a grove of trees, he saw the dryads, who stood gathered in the shade. They were bipeds, with a peculiarly human torso and head structure, though it was clear that they resembled man in only the most superficial style. Their skin was silver, brown, green, in sheens and splotches; the head showed no features other than purplish-green bruises, which seemed to be eye spots. From the shoulders rose members like arms, which branched into twigs and then leaves of dark and pale green, burnished red, bronze-orange, golden ocher. The dryads saw Teehalt and moved forward with almost human interest, then paused about fifty feet distant, swaying on supple limbs, the crests of colored leaves shimmering in the sunlight. They examined Teehalt and he examined them, in a mutual absence of fear, and Teehalt thought them the most entrancing creatures of his experience.

He remembered the days which followed as idyllic, utterly calm. There was a majesty, a clarity, a transcendental qual-

14

ity to the planet, which affected him with an almost religious awe, and presently he came to understand that he must leave shortly or succumb psychically, give himself completely to the world. The knowledge afflicted him with an almost unbearable sadness, for he knew that he would never return.

During this time he watched the dryads as they moved through the valley, idly curious as to their nature and habits. Were they intelligent? Teehalt never answered the question to his own satisfaction. They were wise, certainly —he made this particular distinction. Their metabolism puzzled him, and also the nature of their life cycle, though gradually he acquired at least a glimmer of enlightenment. He assumed, to begin with, that they derived a certain degree of energy from some sort of photosynthetic process.

Then one morning, as Teehalt contemplated a group of dryads standing immobile in the marshy meadow, a large winged hawklike creature swooped down, buffeted one of the dryads to the side. As it toppled Teehalt glimpsed two white shafts, or prongs, extending from the supple gray legs into the ground. The shafts at once retracted when the dryad fell. The hawk creature ignored the toppled dryad, but scratched and tore at the marsh and unearthed an enormous white grub. Teehalt watched with great interest. The dryad apparently had located the grub in its subterranean burrow and had pierced it with a sort of proboscis, presumably for the ingestion of sustenance. Teehalt felt a small pang of shame and disillusionment. The dryads were evidently not quite as innocent and ethereal as he had thought them to be.

The hawk thing lumbered up from the pit, croaked, coughed, flapped away. Teehalt went curiously forward, stared down at the mangled worm. There was little to be seen but shreds of pallid flesh, yellow ooze and a hard black ball, the size of Teehalt's two fists. As he stared down, the dryads came slowly forward and Teehalt withdrew. From a distance he watched as they clustered about the torn worm, and it seemed to Teehalt that they mourned the mangled creature. But presently, with their supple lower limbs, they brought up the black pod and one of them carried it away high in its branches. Teehalt followed at a distance, watched in fascinated wonder as, close beside a grove of slender white-branched trees, the dryads buried the black pod.

In retrospect he wondered why he had attempted no communication with the dryads. Once or twice during the time of his stay he had toyed with the idea, then let the thought drift away—perhaps because he felt himself an intruder, a creature gross and unpleasant. The dryads in their turn treated him with what might be courteous disinterest.

Three days after the black pod had been buried Teehalt had occasion to return to the grove, and to his astonishment saw a pallid shoot rising from the ground above the pod. At the tip pale green leaves already were unfolding into the sunlight. Teehalt stood back, examined the grove with new interest: had each of these trees grown from a pod originated in the body of a subterranean grub? He examined the foliage, limbs, and bark and found nothing to suggest such an origin.

He looked across the valley, to the great dark-leaved giants: surely the two varieties were similar? The giants were majestic, serene, with trunks rising two or three hundred feet to the first branching. The trees grown from the black pods were frail; their foliage was a more tender green, the limbs were more flexible, and branched close to the ground—but the species were clearly related. Leaf shape and structure were almost identical, as was the general appearance of the bark: supple, yet rough-textured, though the bark of the giants was darker and coarser. Teehalt's head swarmed with speculations.

Later the same day he climbed the mountain across the valley and, crossing the ridge, came down upon a glen with precipitous rocky walls. A stream rushed and splashed through mossy boulders and low fernlike plants, falling from pool to pool. Approaching the brink, Teehalt found himself on a level with the foliage of the giant trees, which here grew close beside the cliff. He noted dull green sacs, like fruit, growing among the leaves. Straining, risking a fall, Teehalt was able to pluck one of these sacs. He carried it down the mountainside and across the meadow toward the boat.

He passed a group of dryads who, fixing their purple-green eye bruises on the sac, became rigid. Teehalt observed them with puzzlement. Now they approached, their gorgeous fans quivering and shimmering in agitation. Teehalt felt embarrassed and guilty; evidently by plucking the sac he had offended the dryads. Why or how he could not fathom, but he hastily sought the concealment of his ship, where he cut the sac. The husk was pithy and dry; down the center ran a stalk from which depended white pea-sized seeds, of great complexity. Teehalt inspected the seeds closely under a magnifier. They bore a remarkable resemblance to small underdeveloped beetles, or wasps. With tweezers and knife he

16

opened one out on a sheet of paper, noting wings, thorax, mandibles: clearly an insect.

For a long while he sat contemplating the insects which grew on a tree: a curious analogue, so Teehalt reflected, to the sapling which sprouted from a pod taken from the body of a worm.

Sunset colored the sky; the distant parts of the valley grew indistinct. Dusk came and evening, with the stars blurring large as lamps.

The long night passed. At dawn when Teehalt emerged from his boat he knew that the time of his departure was close at hand. How? Why? He had no answer. The compulsion nevertheless was real; he must leave, and he knew he would never return. As he considered the mother-of-pearl sky, the curve and swell of the hills, the groves and forests, the gentle river, his eyes went damp. The world was too beautiful to leave; far too beautiful to remain upon. It worked on something deep inside him, aroused a queer tumult which he could not understand. There was a constant force from somewhere to run from the ship, to discard his clothes, his weapons, to merge, to envelope and become enveloped, to immolate himself in an ecstacy of identification with beauty and grandeur . . . Today he must go. "If I'm here any longer," thought Teehalt, "I'll be carrying leaves over my head with the dryads."

He wandered up the valley, turning to watch the sun swell into the sky. He climbed to the ridge of the hill, looked east over a succession of rolling crests and valleys, rising gradually to a single great mountain. To west and south he caught the glimmer of water; to the north spread green parkland, with a crumble of gray boulders like the ruins of an ancient city.

Returning into the valley, Teehalt passed below the giant trees. Looking up, he noticed that all the pods had split, and now hung limp and withered. Even as he watched he heard a drone of wings. A hard heavy pellet struck his cheek, where it clung and bit.

In shock and pain Teehalt crushed the insect, or wasp. Looking aloft he saw others—a multitude, darting and veering. Hastily he returned to the ship and dressed in a coverall of tough film. His face and head were protected by transparent mesh. He was unreasonably angry. The wasp's attack had marred his last day in the valley, and in fact had caused him the first pain of his stay. It was too much to expect, he reflected bitterly, that paradise could exist with-

17

out the serpent. And he dropped a can of compressed insect repellent into his pouch, though it might or might not be efficacious against these half-vegetable insects.

Leaving the ship, he marched up the valley, with the insect's bite paining him still. Approaching the forest he came upon a strange scene: a group of dryads surrounded by a buzzing swarm of wasps. Teehalt approached curiously. The dryads, he saw, were under attack, but lacked any efficient means of defense. As the wasps darted in to settle on the silver skin, the dryads flapped their branches, rubbed against each other, scraped with their legs, dislodging the insects as best they could.

Teehalt approached, filled with horrified anger. One of the dryads near him seemed to weaken; several of the insects gnawed through its skin, drawing gouts of ichor. The entire swarm suddenly condensed upon the unfortunate dryad, which tottered and fell, while the remaining dryads moved sedately away.

Teehalt, impelled to disgust and loathing, stepped forward, turned the can of repellent upon the nearly solid mass of wasps. It acted with dramatic effectiveness, the wasps turning white, withering, dropping to the ground; in a single minute the entire swarm was a scatter of small white husks. The dryad under attack also lay dead, having been almost instantly stripped of its flesh. The dryads who had escaped were now returning, and, so Teehalt thought, in a state of anguish and even fury. Their branches quivered and flashed; they marched down upon him with every indication of antagonism. Teehalt took to his heels and returned to his ship.

With binoculars he watched the dryads. They stood about their dead comrade in a state of anxiety and irresolution. Apparently—or at least it seemed so to Teehalt—their anguish was as much for the withered insects as the dead dryad.

They clustered over the fallen body. Teehalt could not observe exactly what they did, but presently they arose with a glossy black ball. He watched them carry it across the valley toward the grove of giant trees.

Chapter 2

I have examined the native life forms of over two thousand planets. I have noted many examples of

18

convergent evolution, but many more of divergence.
... Life, Volume II, by Unspiek, Baron Bodissey.

It is first of all essential that we understand exactly what we mean by the well-used term "convergent evolution." Especially we must not confuse statistical probability with some transcendental and utterly compelling force. Consider the class of all possible objects, the number of which is naturally very large: infinite, indeed, unless we impose an upper and lower limit of mass and certain other physical qualifications. Thus imposing and so qualifying, we find that still only an infinitesimal fraction of this class of objects can be considered life forms.... Before we have even started the investigation we have exercised a very stringent selection of objects which by their very definition will show basic similarities.

To particularize: There are a limited number of methods of locomotion. If we find a quadruped on Planet A, and a quadruped likewise on Planet B, does this imply convergent evolution? No. It merely implies evolution, or perhaps no more than the fact that a four-legged creature can effectively stand without toppling and walk without stumbling. In my opinion, therefore, the expression "convergent evolution" is tautological.

... Ibid.

From: "The Wages of Sin," by Stridenko: article in *Cosmopolis,* May, 1404:

Brinktown: what a city! Once the jumping-off place, the last outpost, the portal into infinity— now just another settlement of the North East Middle Beyond. But "just another?" Is this a fair description? Decidedly not. Brinktown must be seen to be believed, and even then the hard of belief depart incredulous. The houses are set far apart along shaded avenues; still they rise like watchtowers, thrusting up into and through the palms, virebols, scalmettos, and it is a mean house which does not soar above the treetops. The ground level is no more than an entry, a raised pavilion where the clothes must be changed, for local habit ordains the use of paper house capes and paper slippers. Then above: what an explosion of architectural conceits, what turrets and spires, belfries and cupolas! What elaborate magnificence, what inspired scrimshaw, what intricate, inventive, farcical, wonderful applications and misapplications of likely and unlikely materials! Where else can one find balustrades of tortoiseshell studded with gold-plated fish heads? Where else do ivory nymphs hang suspended by their hair from the roof gutters, their faces expressing only bland benediction? Where else can a man's success be gauged by the sumptuousness of the tombstone he designs for himself and erects in his front yard, complete with panegyrical epitaph? And in fact where but in Brinktown is success such an ambiguous recommendation? Few indeed of the inhabitants dare show themselves within the Oikumene. The magistrates are assassins; the civil guard arsonists, extortioners and rapists; the elders of the council, bordello owners. But civic affairs proceed with a punctilio and gravity worthy of the Grand Sessions at Borugstone, or a coronation at the Tower of London. The Brinktown jail is one of the most ingenious ever propounded by civic authorities. It must be remembered that Brinktown occupies the surface of a volcanic butte, overlooking a trackless jungle of quagmire, thorn, eel-vine skiver tussock. A single road leads from city down to jungle; the prisoner is merely locked out of the city. Escape is at his option; he may flee as far through the jungle as he sees fit: the entire continent is at his disposal. But no prisoner ever ventures far from the gate; and, when his presence is required, it is only necessary to unlock the gate and call his name.

*   *   *   *   *   *   *

Teehalt sat looking into the fire. Gersen, vastly touched, wondered if he intended to say more.

At last Teehalt spoke. "So I left the planet. I could stay no longer. To live there a person must either forget himself, give way completely to the beauty, drown his identity in it— or else he must master it, break it, reduce it to a background for his own constructions. I could do neither, so I can never go back.... But the memory of the place haunts me."

"In spite of the wasps?"

Teehalt nodded somberly. "Yes indeed. I did wrong to interfere. There is a rhythm to the planet, an equilibrium which I blundered into and disturbed. I've speculated for days, but I still don't understand the process completely. Wasps are born as fruit of the tree; the worms yield the seed to one kind of tree—this much I know. I suspect that the dryads produce the seed to the great giants. The process of

20

life becomes a great circle, or perhaps a series of incarnations, with the great trees as the end result.

"The dryads seem to tap the worms for part of their sustenance, the wasps devour the dryads. Where do the worms come from? Are the wasps their first phase? Flying larva, so to speak? Do the worms eventually metamorphose into dryads? I feel this must be the case—though I don't know. If so, the cycle is beautiful, in a fashion I can't find words to describe. Something ordained, stately, ancient—like the tides, or the rotation of the galaxy. If the pattern were disturbed, if one link were broken, the whole process would collapse. This would be a great crime."

"So therefore you don't want to reveal the location of the world to your sponsor whom you believe to be Malagate the Woe."

"I *know* to be Malagate," said Teehalt stiffly.

"How did you find out?"

Teehalt looked at him sidewise. "You are very interested in Malagate."

Gersen, wondering if, after all, he were so transparent, shrugged. "One hears many strange tales."

"True. But I do not care to document them. And do you know why?"

"No."

"I have changed my thoughts about you. Now I suspect you of weaselry."

"If I were a weasel," said Gersen, smiling, "I'd hardly admit it. The IPCC has few friends Beyond."

"I am unconcerned," said Teehalt. "But I hope for better days if—when—I return home. I do not care to incur Malagate's animosity by identifying him to a weasel."

"If I were a weasel," said Gersen, "you have already compromised yourself. You know of truth drugs and hypnotic rays."

"Yes. I also know how to avoid them. But no matter; it's not important. You asked how I learned that Malagate was my sponsor. I have no objection to telling you this. It was through my own drunken prolixity. I put into Brinktown. In Sin-San's Tavern I spoke at length, much as I spoke to you tonight, to a dozen enthralled listeners. Yes, I held their attention." Teehalt laughed bitterly. "Presently I was called to the telephone. The man at the other end said his name was Hildemar Dasce. Do you know him?"

"No."

"Odd," said Teehalt, "since you are so interested in Attel

21

Malagate. . . . But, in any event, Dasce spoke to me, told me to report to Smade's. He said I'd meet Malagate here."

"What?" demanded Gersen, unable to control the sharpness of his voice. "Here?"

"Here at Smade's. I asked, what's this to me? I had no dealings with Malagate and wished none. He convinced me otherwise. So I'm here. I am not a brave man." He made a small helpless gesture, picked up his empty glass, looked into it. "I don't know what to do. If I remain Beyond. . . ." Teehalt shrugged.

Gersen considered a moment. "Destroy the monitor filament."

Teehalt shook his head regretfully. "It's the surety I carry for my life. Indeed, I'd rather—" he stopped short. "Did you hear anything?"

Gersen jerked around in his chair. No use denying his nervousness—at least, not to himself. "Rain. Thunder."

"I thought I heard tubes blowing." Teehalt rose to his feet, peered from the window. "Someone is coming."

Gersen also went to the window. "I see nothing."

"A ship dropped down into the field," said Teehalt. He thought for a moment. "There are, or were, only two ships there: yours and the Star King's."

"Where is your ship?"

"I set down in a valley to the north. I want no one meddling with my monitor." He seemed to listen; then, looking into Gersen's eyes, he said, "You are not a locater."

"No."

Teehalt nodded. "Locaters are, by and large, a vile lot. You are not of the IPCC?"

"Think of me as an explorer."

"Will you help me?"

The harsh precepts of Gersen's training contended with his impulses. He muttered ungraciously, "Within limits—very narrow limits."

Teehalt smiled thinly. "What are these limits?"

"My own business is urgent. I can't allow myself to be diverted."

Teehalt was neither disappointed nor resentful; he could expect no more from a stranger. "Odd," he said once more, "that you do not know Hildemar Dasce—sometimes known as Beauty Dasce. But he will come in presently. You ask, how do I know? By the logic of plain ordinary fear."

"You'll be safe so long as you stay inside the tavern," said Gersen shortly. "Smade has his rules."

22

Teehalt nodded, politely acknowledging the discomfiture he had caused Gersen. A minute passed. The Star King rose to his feet, his pink and red garment glowing in the firelight. He walked slowly up the stairs, looking neither to right nor left.

Teehalt followed him with his eyes. "Impressive creature. ... I understand that only the handsome ones are allowed to leave their planet."

"So I have heard."

Teehalt sat looking into the fire. Gersen started to speak, then restrained himself. He felt exasperation with Teehalt, for a clear and simple reason: Teehalt had aroused his sympathy, Teehalt had entered his mind, Teehalt had burdened him with new troubles. He also felt dissatisfaction with himself—for reasons by no means so simple, in fact for no rational reason whatever. Beyond argument, his own affairs were of paramount importance; he could not permit himself to be diverted. If emotion and sentiment could sway him so easily, where would such things stop?

The dissatisfaction, far from being appeased, grew more insistent. There was a connection, too tenuous to be defined, with the world Teehalt had described; a sense of loss and longing, of some indefinable inadequacy.... Gersen made a sudden angry motion, swept all the irritating doubts and questions from his mind. They could only decrease his effectiveness.

Five minutes passed. Teehalt reached into his jacket, brought forth an envelope. "Here are photographs you might be pleased to inspect at your leisure."

Gersen took them without comment.

The door slid back. Three dark shapes stood in the gap, looking into the room. Smade roared from behind the bar, "Come in or stay out! Must I warm the whole cursed planet?"

Into the hall stepped the strangest human being of Gersen's experience. "And there," said Teehalt with a sick titter, "you see Beauty Dasce."

Dasce was about six feet tall. His torso was a tube, the same gauge from knee to shoulder. His arms were thin and long, terminating in great bony wrists, enormous hands. His head was also tall and round, with a ruff of red hair, and a chin seeming almost to rest on the clavicle. Dasce had stained his neck and face bright red, excepting only his cheeks, which were balls of bright chalk-blue, like a pair of mildewed oranges. At some stage of his career his nose had been cleft into a pair of cartilaginous prongs, and his eyelids had been cut

23

away; to moisten his corneas he wore two nozzles connected to a tank of fluid which every few seconds discharged a film of mist into his eyes. There was also a pair of shutters, now raised, which could be lowered to cover his eyes from the light, and which were painted to represent staring white and blue eyes similar to Dasce's own.

The two men at his back by contrast appeared ordinary run-of-the-mill human beings: both dark, hard, competent-seeming, with quick clever eyes.

Dasce made a brusque signal to Smade, who stood impassively watching from behind the bar. "Three rooms, if you please. We will eat presently."

"Very well."

"The name is Hildemar Dasce."

"Very well, Mr. Dasce."

Dasce now sauntered across the room to where Teehalt and Gersen sat. His glance shifted from one to the other. "Since we are fellow travelers, houseguests of Mr. Smade, let us introduce ourselves," he said politely. "My name is Hildemar Dasce. May I inquire yours?"

"I am Kirth Gersen."

"I am Keelen Tannas."

Dasce's lips, pale purple-gray against the red of his skin, moved in a smile. "To an amazing degree you resemble a certain Lugo Teehalt whom I expected to find here."

"Think of me as you like," said Teehalt in a reedy voice. "I have spoken my name."

"But what a pity; I have business to transact with Lugo Teehalt!"

"It is pointless, then, to approach me."

"As you wish. Though I suspect that the business with Lugo Teehalt might interest Keelen Tannas. Will you step aside for a moment's private conversation?"

"No. I am not interested. My friend knows my name; it is Keelen Tannas."

"Your 'friend'?" Dasce turned his attention to Gersen. "Do you know this man well?"

"As well as I know anyone."

"And his name is Keelen Tannas?"

"If this is the name he offers you, I suggest that you accept it."

Without further remark Dasce turned away. He and his men went to a table at the end of the hall, where they ate.

Teehalt spoke in a hollow voice. "He knows me well enough."

24

Gersen felt a new spasm of irritation. Why should Teehalt feel impelled to embroil a stranger in his troubles, if his identity were already known?

Teehalt explained his act in the next breath. "Since I fight the hook, he thinks he has me trapped, and he amuses himself."

"What of Malagate? I thought you had come here to meet him."

"Better that I return to Alphanor and confront him there. I will return his money, but I will not lead him to the planet."

At the end of the hall Dasce and his two companions were served with platters from Smade's kitchen. Gersen watched them for a moment. "They seem unconcerned."

Teehalt sniffed. "They think that I will deal with Malagate, but not with them. . . . I will try to escape. Dasce does not know that I landed over the hill. Perhaps he thinks that your ship is mine."

"Who are the other two men?"

"Assassins. They know me well enough, from the tavern at Brinktown. Tristano is an Earthman. He kills by touches of his hand. The other is a Sarkoy venefice. He can brew stuff to kill from sand and water. All three are madmen—but Dasce is the worst. He knows every horror there is to be known."

At this moment Dasce looked at his watch. Wiping his mouth with the back of his hand, he rose, crossed the room, bent over Teehalt. In a husky whisper he said, "Attel Malagate waits you outside. He will see you now."

Teehalt stared at him with sagging jaw. Dasce swaggered back to his table.

Teehalt rubbed his face with quivering fingers, turned to Gersen. "I can still evade them if I can lose myself in the dark. When I run out the door, will you detain these three?"

"How do you suggest I do this?" asked Gersen sardonically.

Teehalt was silent a moment. "I don't know."

"Nor do I, with the best will in the world."

Teehalt gave a sad nod. "Very well, then. I will fend for myself. Goodby, Mr. Gersen."

He rose to his feet, walked to the bar. Dasce slanted his eyes at him, but otherwise seemed uninterested. Beside the bar, Teehalt stood beyond the reach of his vision, whereupon he darted into the kitchen, out of sight. Smade looked after him with wonder, then returned to business.

Dasce and the two assassins stolidly continued their meal.

Gersen watched covertly. Why did they sit with such unconcern? Teehalt's ruse had been pitifully obvious. Gersen's

25

skin began to prickle; he drummed his fingers on the table. In spite of his resolve, he rose to his feet, went to the doorway. Pushing open the timber panels, he stepped out on the veranda.

The night was dark, lit only by stars. The wind, for a wonder, was still; but the sea, swirling and flowing, sent up a muffled sad sound. . . . A short sharp cream, a whimper, from behind the tavern. Gersen abandoned his resolve and started forward. A grip like the pinch of steel seized his arm, tweaked nerves at the back of his elbow; another hand clamped at his neck. Gersen let himself fall, broke the grip. Suddenly all his doubts and exasperations were gone; he was a whole man. He rolled over, bounced to his feet, stood in a half crouch, shuffled slowly forward. Facing him with an easy smile stood Tristano the Earthman.

"Careful, friend," said Tristano in the clipped flat Earth accent. "Give me trouble and Smade pitches you into the sea."

Dasce came out the door, followed by the Sarcoy poisoner. Tristano joined them and the three walked to the spaceport. Gersen remained on the terrace, breathing heavily, crawling internally with his frustraded need for action.

Ten minutes later two ships rose into the night. The first was a squat armored vessel, with weapons fore and aft. The second was a battered old locater's ship, Model 9B.

Gersen stared in wonder. The second ship was his own.

The ships disappeared; the sky once more was empty. Gersen returned into the tavern and sat before the fire. Presently he brought forth the envelope given him by Lugo Teehalt, opened it, and extracted three photographs, which he examined for the better part of an hour.

The fire burnt low; Smade took himself off to bed, leaving a son dozing behind the bar. Outside, the night rains began to thrash down, lightning crackled, the ocean groaned.

Gersen sat in deep thought. Presently from his pocket he brought a sheet of paper, which listed five names:

> Attel Malagate (the Woe)
> Howard Alan Treesong
> Viole Falushe
> Kokor Hekkus (the Killing Machine)
> Lens Larque

From his pocket he brought a pencil, but still he deliberated. If he continually added names to his list he would never finish. Of course there was no real need to write; there was no real need for a list: Gersen knew the five names as well as he knew his own. He compromised. To the right and below the last name of the original list he appended a sixth: Hildemar Dasce. For a space he sat looking at the names, with two sides to his mind: the one so alive and passionate that the other, the cerebral detached observer, felt a trace of amusement.

The flames settled low; chunks of fossilized moss glowed scarlet; the sea sound was slower and lower in pitch. Gersen rose to his feet, climbed the stone stairs to his room.

During his life Gersen had known little other than a succession of strange beds; nevertheless sleep came slowly and he lay staring into the dark. Visions passed before him, from as early as he could remember. First there was a landscape which, as he recalled it, was wonderfully pleasant and bright. There were tawny mountains, a village painted in faded pastel colors along the banks of a wide tawny river.

But this picture, as always, was followed by another even more vivid: the same landscape littered with hacked and bleeding bodies. Men and women and children shuffled into the holds of five long ships under the weapons of two score men in strange grim costumes. With an old man who was his grandfather, Kirth Gersen watched, horrified, from across the river, concealed from the slavers by the bulk of an old barge. When the ships had lifted, they returned across the river to the silence of death. Then his grandfather told him, "Many fine things your father had planned for you: learning and useful work and a life of satisfaction and peace. Do you recall this?"

"Yes, Grandfather."

"The learning you shall have. You will learn patience and resource, the ability of your hands and your mind. You will have useful work: the destruction of evil men. What work could be more useful? This is Beyond; you will find that your work is never done—so therefore you may never know a life of peace. However, I guarantee you ample satisfaction, for I will teach you to crave the blood of these men more than the flesh of woman."

The old man had been as good as his word. Eventually they made their way to Earth, the ultimate repository of every sort of knowledge.

Young Kirth learned many things, from a succession of strange teachers which it would be tedious to detail. He killed his first man at the age of fourteen, a footpad who had the ill-luck to accost them in a back alley of Rotterdam. While his grandfather stood by, in the manner of an old fox teaching

27

a cub to hunt, young Kirth, gasping and sobbing, broke first the ankle, then the neck of the astonished assailant.

From Earth they moved to Alphanor, capitol planet of the Rigel Concourse, and here Kirth Gersen gained more conventional knowledge. When he was nineteen his grandfather died, bequeathing him a comfortable sum of money and a letter which read:

My dear Kirth:

I have seldom told of my affection and high regard for you; I take this occasion to do so. You have come to mean more to me than ever did my own son. I will not say I am sorry that I have set your feet in the path they now must take, even though you will be denied many ordinary pleasures and luxuries. Have I been presumptuous in so shaping your life? I think not. For several years you have been self-motivated, and have showed no inclination to point yourself in any other direction. In any event, I can think of no more useful service for a man to perform than that which I have ordained for you. The Law of Man is bounded by the limits of the Oikumene. Good and evil, however, are ideas which encompass the universe; unluckily, beyond the Pale there are few to ensure the triumph of good over evil.

Actually the triumph consists of two processes: first evil must be extinguished, then good must be introduced to fill the gap. It is impossible that a man should be equally efficacious in both functions. Good and evil, in spite of a traditional fallacy, are not polarities, nor mirror images, nor is one merely the absence of the other. In order to minimize confusion, your work will be the destruction of evil men.

What is an evil man? The man is evil who coerces obedience to his private ends, destroys beauty, produces pain, extinguishes life. It must be remembered that killing evil men is not equivalent to expunging evil, which is a relationship between a situation and an individual. A poisonous spore will grow only in a nutrient soil. In this case the nutrient soil is Beyond, and since no human effort can alter the Beyond (which must always exist), you must devote your efforts to destroying the poisonous spores, which are evil men. It is a task of which you will never see the end.

Our sharpest and first motivation in this matter,

agreed, is no more than a primitive ache for revenge. Five pirate captains destroyed certain lives and enslaved others who were precious to us. Revenge is not an ignoble motive, when it works to a productive end. The names of these five pirate captains I do not know. My best attempts have brought me no information. One man, an underling, I recognized: his name is Parsifal Pankarow, and he is no less baneful than the five captains, though his potentialities for harm are less. You must seek him Beyond and learn from him the names of the five.

Then you must kill the five, and it will do no harm if they suffer pain in the process, for they have brought an immeasurable amount of pain and grief to others.

There is still much for you to learn. I would advise you to join the Institute, except I fear that the disciplines of this body would not set well with you. Do as you think best. In my youth I thought to become a catechumen, but Destiny ruled otherwise. If I were friends with a Fellow I would send you to him for counsel—but I have no such friend. Perhaps you will be less constricted outside the Institute. Stringent conditions are imposed upon the catechumen through the first fourteen degrees.

In any event, I advise you to devote a time to the study of Sarkoy poisons and hand techniques, preferably on Sarkovy itself. There is room for improvement in your marksmanship and knifeplay, though you need fear few men at hand fighting. Your intuitive judgments are good; your self-control, economy of action, and versatility are to be commended. But you still have much to learn. For the next ten years, study, train—and be cautious. There are many other capable men; do not rashly waste yourself against any such until you are more than ready. In short, do not make an overvirtue of courage or heroism. A goodly amount of caution—call it fear or even cowardice—is a highly desirable adjunct for a man such as yourself, whose one fault might be said to be a mystical, almost superstitious, faith in the success of your destiny. Do not be fooled: we are all mortal, as I now attest.

So, my grandson, I am dead. I have trained you to know good from evil. I feel only pride in my accomplishment, and hope that you will remember me with affection and respect.

Your loving grandfather,
Rolf Marr Gersen

29

For eleven years Kirth Gersen obeyed the dictates of his grandfather, or exceeded them, meanwhile seeking both within the Oikumene and Beyond for Parsifal Pankarow, but fruitlessly.

Few occupations offered more challenge, more hazard, more chilling rebuffs to incompetence than weaseling for the IPCC. Gersen undertook two assignments, on Pharode and Blue Planet. During the term of this latter, he submitted a preemptive requisition for information regarding Parsifal Pankarow, and felt himself well rewarded to learn that Parsifal Pankarow currently resided at Brinktown, where he was Ira Bugloss, operator of a prosperous import business.

Gersen found Ira Bugloss, or Pankarow, to be a burly, hearty man, egg-bald, his skin dyed lemon-yellow, his mustachios wide, black and luxuriant.

Brinktown occupied a plateau which stood like an island in a black-and-orange jungle. Gersen scrutinized Pankarow's movements for two weeks, and learned his routine, which was that of a man without a care. Then one evening he hired a cab, rendered the operator unconscious, and waited outside the Jodisei Conversation and Flower Arranging Club until Pankarow tired of sporting with the inmates and emerged into the humid Brinktown night. Well pleased with himself, humming a tune he had only just learned, he staggered into the cab and was conveyed, not to his sumptuous home, but to a remote clearing in the jungle. Here Gersen put questions which Pankarow had no wish to answer.

Pankarow made an effort to hold his tongue, to no avail. Finally five names were wrung from his memory. "Now what will you do with me?" croaked the erstwhile Ira Bugloss.

"I will kill you," said Gersen, pale and quivering after exercise he did not enjoy. "I have made you my enemy; furthermore, you deserve to die a hundred times over."

"At one time, yes " cried the sweating Pankarow. "Now I lead a blameless life; I injure no one!"

Gersen wondered if every such occasion would cause him such nausea, misgivings and misery. He responded in a voice held crisp and even by enormous effort. "What you say perhaps is true, but your wealth stinks of pain. And certainly you will make a report to the first agent of any of the five you meet."

"No. I swear not. And my wealth—take it all."

"Where is your wealth?"

Pankarow tried to make conditions. "I will lead you to it."

Gersen shook his head sadly. "Accept my excuses. You are

about to die. It comes to all men; you had best feel that you are requiting the evil you have done—"

"Under my tombstone!" screamed Pankarow. "Under the stone tombstone before my house!"

Gersen touched a tube to Pankarow's neck, which spat a Sarkoy poison into the skin. "I will go to look," he said. "You will sleep until you see me again." Gersen spoke no more than the truth. Pankarow relaxed thankfully and was dead in seconds.

Gersen returned to Brinktown, a deceptively placid settlement of tall ornate three-, four-, and five-story houses embowered among green, purple and black trees. At twilight he sauntered along a quiet back lane to Pankarow's house. The stone tombstone stood plain to see: a massive monument of marble spheres and cubes surmounted by a sculptured image of Parsifal Pankarow in a noble pose, head thrown back to the sky, arms outspread. As Gersen stood appraising it a boy thirteen or fourteen years old stepped down from the porch and approached Gersen.

"Are you from my father? Is he with the fat women?"

Gersen steeled his heart to the inevitable pangs, and put aside all thought of confiscating Pankarow's wealth. "I bring a message from your father."

"Will you come in?" inquired the boy, tremulously anxious. "I'll call my mother."

"No. Please don't. I have no time. Listen carefully. Your father has been called away. He is not sure when he can return. Perhaps never."

The boy listened round-eyed. "Did he—run away?"

Gersen nodded. "Yes. Some old enemies found him, and he does not dare show himself. He said to tell you or your mother that money is hidden under the tombstone."

The boy stared at Gersen. "Who are you?"

"A messenger, no more. Tell your mother exactly what I have told you. One more thing: when you look beneath the tombstone, be careful. There may be a trap to guard the money. Do you understand what I'm saying?"

"Yes. A booby trap."

"That's right. Be careful. Get the help of someone you can trust."

Gersen departed Brinktown. He thought of Smade's Planet, with its elemental quiet and isolation, precisely the antidote to his fretful conscience. Where, he asked himself, as the locater boat skidded down a fracture in the continuum, did the balance lie? He had by no means reached the tipping point:

31

Parsifal Pankarow deserved the callous execution he had received. But what of wife and son? They must bear the pain, but why? To protect the women and children of more deserving men from worse...so Gersen reassured himself. But the haunted dark look of the boy's eyes would not leave his memory.

Destiny led him. The first at Smade's Tavern engaged him with Malagate the Woe, the first name Parsifal Pankarow had blurted forth. In his bed Gersen heaved a deep sigh. Pankarow was dead; poor miserable Lugo Teehalt was probably dead. All men must die; let there be an end to brooding. He grinned into the dark, thinking of Malagate and Beauty Dasce examining the monitor of his ship. To begin with they would be unable to open the monitor with their key—a formidable difficulty, even worse if they suspected thief-proofing of explosive, poison gas or acid. When after great travail they eventually extracted the filament, it would show blank. Gersen's monitor was no more than window dressing; he had never bothered to activate it.

Malagate would look questioningly at Beauty Dasce, who would mutter some sort of objurgation. Perhaps then they would think to check the serial number of the ship, only to find that it was different from that issued to Lugo Teehalt. And then: swiftly back to Smade's Planet. But Gersen would be gone.

Chapter 3

Question (put to Eale Maurmath, Chief Quaestor of Tri-Planetary Police System, during a round-table television discussion broadcast from Conover, Cuthbert, Vega. May 16, 993):
I know your problems are tremendous, Quaestor Maurmath, in fact I don't really comprehend how you get on top of them. For instance, how can you possibly locate some one particular man, or trace his background, among ninety-odd inhabited planets and billions of people, of all varieties of political complexion, local habit, doctrines of belief?
Answer:
Usually we can't.

Message of Lord Jaiko Jaikoska, Chairman of the Executive Board, to the Valhalla General Legislative Assembly, Valhalla, Tau Gemini, August 9, 1028:

I urge you not to endorse this sinister measure. Humanity many times has had sad experience of superpowerful police forces...As soon as (the police) slip out from under the firm thumb of a suspicious local tribune, they become arbitrary, merciless, a law unto themselves. They think no more of justice, but only of establishing themselves as a privileged and envied elite. They mistake the attitude of natural caution and uncertainty of the civilian population as admiration and respect, and presently they start to swagger back and forth, jingling their weapons in megalomaniac euphoria. People thereupon become not masters, but servants. Such a police force becomes merely an aggregate of uniformed criminals, the more baneful in that their position is unchallenged and sanctioned by law. The police mentality cannot regard a human being in terms other than as an item or object to be processed as expeditiously as possible. Public convenience or dignity means nothing; police prerogatives assume the status of divine law. Submissiveness is demanded. If a police officer kills a civilian, it is a regrettable circumstance: the officer was possibly overzealous. If a civilian kills a police officer all hell breaks loose. The police foam at the mouth. All other business comes to a standstill until the perpetrator of this most dastardly act is found out. Inevitably, when apprehended, he is beaten or otherwise tortured for his intolerable presumption. The police complain that they cannot function efficiently, that criminals escape them. Better a hundred unchecked criminals than the despotism of one unbridled police force. Again I warn you, do not endorse this measure. If you do, I shall surely veto it.

Excerpt from address of Richard Parnell, Commissioner of Public Weal, Northern Territory, Xion, Rigel Concourse, to the Association of Police Officers, Civil Guards and Crime Detection Agencies, at Parilia, Pilgham, Rigel, December 1, 1075:

...It is not enough to say that our problems are unique; they have become catastrophic. We are held responsible for the efficient conduct of our jobs, but are refused the necessary tools and powers to do so. A man can murder and rob anywhere within the

Oikumene, jump into a waiting spaceship and be light years away before his crime is discovered. If he passes beyond the Pale, our jurisdiction ends—at least officially, although all of us know of courageous officers who have put justice ahead of expediency and caution and have gone beyond the Pale to make their arrests. This of course they have a right to do, since every human law becomes invalid Beyond, but the risk is their own.

More often the criminal who goes Beyond escapes scot free. When he chooses to return into the Oikumene he may have changed his appearance, his LOSI coordinates, and his fingerprints, and is safe unless he has the misfortune to be arrested for a new infraction in the community where he committed his original crime and was there genified.*

Essentially, in this day of the Jarnell Intersplit, any criminal who takes a few elementary precautions can go unpunished.

This association many times has sought to establish a more satisfactory basis for crime detection and prevention. Our main problem is the diversity of local police organizations, with their totally disparate standards, goals, and range of problems, and the consequent chaos of information files and retrieval systems. An obvious solution exists, and the association's standing recommendation is the formation of a single official police system to maintain law and order throughout the Oikumene.

The advantages of such a system are obvious: standardization of procedure, use of new equipment and ideas, unified control, a central office for the filing, indexing, and cross-indexing of information, and, perhaps of highest importance, the creation and maintenance of an *esprit*, a pride of profession, to attract and hold men and women of the highest abilities.

As we all know, this centralized agency has been denied us, no matter how urgently we plead its virtues. The ostensible motive behind this refusal is known to us all, and I will not dignify it by mentioning it. I will say that police morale is sinking to an ever lower level and soon may vanish—unless something is done.

Today I wish to put before the convention a proposal for the "something." Our association is the

*The noun is *gene-classification*, thence to adjective *gene-classified*, abbreviated to *genified*.

34

private organization of a group of private individuals. It has no official status or connection with any governmental office whatever. In short, we are free to do what we please, enter into any kind of business we please, so long as we contravene no laws.

I propose that this association go into business, that we found a private crime-detection agency. The new company will be strictly a commercial proposition, financed by association money and by private subscription. Headquarters will be established at some central and convenient location, but there will be branches on every planet. Our staff will be recruited from among members of this association and any other qualified persons. They will be well paid, from fees and profits. Where will these fees and profits derive? Primarily from local police organizations, who will use certain of the facilities of this new interplanetary agency, instead of expending large sums to maintain redundant facilities of the same sort. Since the proposed agency will be a private business organization subject to all local and interplanetary laws, the critics of our former schemes must be silenced.

... Eventually the Interworld Police Coordination here the IPCC may function usefully. In due course Company would automatically be called upon to handle all problems of crime detection and prevention other than those that are purely local, and even the IPCC will certainly dwarf in scope all present and future official police groups. We will have our own laboratories, research programs, absolutely complete files, and an absolutely high-class staff—recruited, as I say, from members of the association, and others. Are there any questions?

Question from the floor: Is there any reason why police officers of a municipality or a state should not simultaneously be members of the IPCC staff?

Answer: This is a very important point. No, there is no reason. I see no conflict between the two agencies, and there is every reason to hope that local police officials will automatically wish to become affiliated with the IPCC. This would be to the advantage of the IPCC, the local police group, and the individual himself. In other words, the local police officer would have nothing to lose and everything to gain by referring cases to the IPCC and authorizing the subsequent fee if he himself were a staff member.

From Chapter III, *The IPCC: Men and Methods,*
by Raoul Past:

...Nominally an intra-Oikumene organ, the IPCC
has been forced by the dynamics of its basic rationale
to operate Beyond. Here, where the only laws are
local ordinances and taboos, the IPCC finds little
cooperation: indeed, the very opposite. The IPCC
operative is known as a weasel; his life is constantly
balanced on a knife edge. The Central Agency
shrouds in secrecy the exact number of "weasels,"
and also the percentage of casualties. The first figure
is suspected to be low, through difficulties of re-
cruitment; the second high, through both the exi-
gencies of the work and the efforts of that most
fantastic of human constructions, the Deweaseling
Corps.

...The universe is infinite; worlds without end
exist; but certainly one must travel far to find a
situation so paradoxical, whimsical, and grim as
this: that the single disciplined organization of the
Beyond exists only to extirpate the nominal forces
of law and order.

* * * * * * *

Gersen awoke in the strange bed, the sky through the small
square window only vaguely gray. He dressed and descended
the stone steps to the hall, where he found one of Smade's
sons, a dour dark lad of twelve, fanning the coals in the fire-
place to life. He bade Gersen a gruff "Good morning," but
seemed indisposed for further conversation. Gersen stepped
outside to the terrace. Predawn mist concealed the ocean,
rolling in sheets and curls across the heath—a dreary, mono-
chromatic scene. The sense of isolation was suddenly oppres-
sive. Gersen returned inside, went to warm himself at the
new fire.

The boy was sweeping the hearth. "Killing last night," he
told Gersen in gloomy satisfaction. "Little thin man got it.
Right behind the moss shed."

"Is the body there?" Gersen asked.

"No. No body. They took it with them. Three bad ones,
maybe four. Father is black mad; they did their dirt inside
the fence."

Gersen grunted, displeased with every aspect of the situation. He asked for breakfast, which was presently forthcoming.
As he ate, the dwarf sun lifted above the mountains, a brittle
white wafer barely visible through the mist. An onshore wind
came up, the mist dissipated; and when Gersen once more

36

went outside the sky was clear, though fog wisps still blew in from the oily sea.

Gersen walked north along the shelf between ocean cliffs and mountains. Underfoot was a carpet of spongy gray moss, redolent with a musty resinous odor. The sunlight streamed over his head, out to sea, the black water giving back no glint or reflection. He went to the edge of the cliff, looked down two hundred feet to the rise and fall of the water. He tossed a stone, watched the splash, the ripples quickly absorbed in the larger motion. What would it be like, he wondered, to sail a boat on this ocean? Out across the horizons, with the whole world to explore: barren coasts, bleak headlands, tall stern islands, with no sight of human being or dwelling until the return to Smade's Tavern. Gersen turned away from the cliff, continued North. He passed the mouth of a valley fenced in against Smade's cattle. Teehalt certainly had not left his boat here. A quarter mile ahead a spur of the mountains humped down almost to the sea. In the shadow of the ridge Gersen found Teehalt's boat.

He made a quick inspection. The vessel was indeed a Model 9B, identical to his own. The gear and machinery seemed in good order. In a housing under the bow bulge hung the monitor which had cost Teehalt his life.

Gersen returned to the tavern. His original plan, to spend several days, must be altered; Malagate might discover his mistake and return with Hildemar Dasce and the two assassins. They would wish to take Teehalt's monitor, and this Gersen was resolved they should not do, though he did not care to risk his life in the effort to keep it.

Returning to the tavern, he noted that the landing field was empty. The Star King had departed. This morning? Or during the night? Gersen had no idea. He settled his score and, moved by some obscure impulse, paid Lugo Teehalt's bill. Smade made no comment. He was clearly consumed by cold fury. His eyes showed white around the drab irises, his nostrils were distended, his chin jutted forward. The rage was not on Lugo Teehalt's behalf, Gersen realized; the murderer, whoever he might be—Dasce had mentioned Attel Malagate—had flouted Smade's law; he had disturbed the serenity of Smade's Tavern; he had wronged Smade. Gersen felt a twinge of sad amusement, which he took pains to conceal. Politely he inquired, "When did the Star King leave?" Smade merely glared silently back at him like an angry Black Angus bull.

Gersen gathered his small packet of belongings and departed the tavern, declining the twelve-year-old boy's proffer of assistance. Once more he walked north across the gray heath. Crossing the ridge, he looked back toward the tavern. Staunch and secure it stood, facing the black, wind-whipped sea—utterly alone. Gersen shook his head dubiously and turned away. "Everyone is the same," he told himself. Anxious to arrive and, when they leave, wondering why they came."

A few minutes later he took Teehalt's boat aloft on its boosters, then pointed it back toward the Oikumene and cut in the oversplit. Smade's Planet dwindled astern and, with its white dwarf sun, presently became lost, a single spark among a million. Stars slid by like fireflies blown on a dark wind, the light reaching Gersen by backsplash or backcurl, wherein the Döppler effect played no role. Perspective was lost; the eye was fooled; stars moved astern, the near slipping across the far. Within hand reach? A hundred yards distant? Ten miles? The eye had no tool by which to judge.

Gersen set the star finder to the index of Rigel, engaged the autopilot, made himself as comfortable as the spartan facilities of the Model 9B permitted.

The visit to Smade's Tavern had served him well, though the occasion had been bought by Lugo Teehalt's death. Malagate wanted Lugo Teehalt's monitor; this was the premise which controlled the shape of the future. Malagate would be willing to enter negotiations, and, with equal certainty, he would act through an agent. Although, thought Gersen, he had seen fit to kill Lugo Teehalt at first hand. . . . There was something puzzling here. Why need Lugo Teehalt die? Sheer malice on the part of Malagate? Not impossible. But Malagate had killed and ravaged so extensively that taking the life of one thin miserable man could provide him only paltry gratification.

More likely the motive was habit, sheer offhanded casual habit. To sever relations with a man who might be inconvenient, you killed him. . . . A third possibility: Had Teehalt penetrated the anonymity which Malagate, among all the Demon Princes, held of supreme inportance? Gersen reviewed his conversation with Teehalt. For all his ravaged and woebegone appearance, Teehalt had used educated intonations. He had seen better days. Why had he turned to the disreputable profession of locating? The question, of course, had no real answer. Why did a man set himself in any specific direction? Why and how did a man, presumably born of ordinary parents, become Attel Malagate the Woe?

Teehalt had hinted or implied that Malagate was somehow

38

involved in the leasing of the locater ship. With this thought in mind, Gersen made a careful inspection of the ship. He found the traditional brass plate naming the place of manufacture: Liverstone on Fiame, a planet of the Rigel Concourse. The monitor likewise carried a bronze flake detailing its serial number and the manufacturer: the Feritse Precision Instruments Company, at Sansontiana on Olliphane, also of the Concourse. But there was no indication of the owner, no evidence of registration.

It would be necessary, then, to trace ownership of the boat indirectly. Gersen set himself to consider the problem. Estate houses maintained two-thirds of all locater ships, their stock in trade consisting of worlds with specific attributes: planets highly mineralized, planets suitable for colonization by dissident groups, planets pleasant enough to serve as a millionaire's reserve, planets distinguished by a sufficiently interesting flora and fauna to attract curio dealers or biologists; most rarely, planets supporting intelligent or semi-intelligent life, of interest to sociologists, cultural taxonomists, linguists, and the like.

The estate houses were concentrated in the cosmopolitan centers of the Oikumene: three or four worlds of the Concourse, chief among them Alphanor; Vega's Cuthbert, Boniface, Aloysius; Noval; Pi Cassiopeia's Copus and Orpo; Quantique; old Earth. The Concourse would be the logical starting place, if in fact Lugo Teehalt worked for an estate house. But this was by no means certain; in fact, as Gersen seemed to recall, Teehalt had implied otherwise. If so, the investigation was narrowed considerably. Next to the estate houses, universities and research institutes were the chief employers of locaters. And Gersen had a new thought. If Teehalt had been either a student or a faculty member at some specific lyceum, college or university, he would probably apply to this same institution for employment.

Gersen corrected his thinking: the conjecture was not necessarily probable. A proud man, with friends and associates who might remember him, would use his old school in this fashion only as a last resort. Was Lugo Teehalt proud? Not in this way, or so it seemed to Gersen. Teehalt had seemed a man who might easily turn to his old haven for security.

There was another obvious source of information: the Feritse Precision Instrument Company at Sansontiana, where the monitor would be registered in the name of its purchaser. And another reason for visiting the Feritse Precison Instrument Company: Gersen wanted to open the monitor and remove the filament. To this end he needed a key. Monitors were often tamperproofed with explosive capsules or corrosives; violent extraction of the filament seldom yielded useful information.

The officials of the Feritse Company might or might not prove accommodating. Sansontiana was a city of Braichis, one of Olliphane's nineteen independent nations; the Braichish were a headstrong, involute, altogether peculiar people. Concourse law, however, repudiated private claims beyond the Pale, and discouraged the use of explosive traps. Hence, in an ordinance detailing the equipment required aboard spacecraft: "The manufacturers of such devices (referring to monitors) are thereupon enjoined and required to furnish keys, switching devices, code sticks, number sequences or any other tool, appliance or information necessary to the safe opening of the instrument in question, without delay, complaint, error, exorbitant charge, or any behavior or act calculated to deter the petitioner from obtaining the key, coded device or information demanded, if and when the petitioner is able to demonstrate ownership of said instrument. Presentation of the serial plate originally or thereafter affixed by the manufacturer to the instrument shall be deemed sufficient and adequate evidence of ownership."

All well and good. Gersen could secure the key, but the company need not furnish information as to previous registration of the instrument. Especially if Attel Malagate should suspect that Gersen might come to Sansontiana with such a purpose in mind, and take steps to preclude the contingency.

The thought opened a set of new vistas. Gersen frowned. Had his temperament been other than careful and orderly, these various options and possibilities might not occur to him. He would be saved a great deal of difficulty, but he probably would die sooner. . . . He shook his head in resignation, reached for the star charts.

Not far off his line of fission was the star Cygnus T342, and its planet Euville where an unpleasant and psychotic population lived in five cities: Oni, Me, Che, Dun and Ve, each compulsively built in pentagonal patterns, from a central five-sided citadel. The spaceport, on a remote island, was opprobriously named "Orifice." Everything Gersen needed could be found at the spaceport; he had no desire to visit the cities, especially since each required, in lieu of passport, the tattooing of a star on the forehead, a different color for each city. To visit all five cities the prospective tourist must display five stars: orange, black, mauve, yellow and green.

Chapter 4

From *New Discoveries in Space*, by Ralph Quarry:

...Sir Julian Hove apparently derived his attitudes from the late Renaissance explorers. Upon return to Earth, members of his crews imposed upon themselves (or had imposed) a strict rule of discretion and secrecy. Details nevertheless leaked out. Sir Julian Hove was, to use the most comprehensive term, a martinet. He was likewise a man utterly without humor. His eye was bleak, he spoke without moving his lips; his hair was combed day after day in photographically indentical furrows. While he did not actually require that the personnel wear dinner jackets to meals, certain of his rules imposed an almost equivalent punctilio.... The use of first names was eschewed; salutes were exchanged at the beginning and termination of each watch, even though the personnel was by and large civilian. Technicians whose specialties were without scientific pertinence were forbidden to set foot on the fascinating new worlds: an order which came close to fomenting mutiny, until Sir Julian's second in command, Howard Coke, prevailed upon Sir Julian to ameliorate this regulation.

The Rigel Concourse is Sir Julian's most noteworthy discovery: twenty-six magnificent planets, most of them not only habitable but salubrious, though only two display even quasi-intelligent autochthones.... Sir Julian, exercising his prerogatives, named the planets for boyhood heroes: *Lord Kitchener, William Gladstone, Archbishop Rollo Gore, Edythe MacDevott, Rudyard Kipling, Thomas Carlyle, William Kircudbright, Samuel B. Gorsham, Sir Robert Peel*, and the like.

But Sir Julian was to be deprived of his privilege. He telegraphed ahead the news of his return to Maudley Space Station, together with a description of the Concourse and the names he had bestowed upon the members of this magnificent group. The list passed through the hands of an obscure young clerk, one Roger Pilgham, who rejected Sir Julian's nominations in disgust. To each of the twenty-six

41

planets he assigned a letter of the alphabet and hurriedly supplied new names: Alphanor, Barleycorn, Chrysanthe, Diogenes, Elfland, Fiame, Goshen, Hardacres, Image, Jezebel, Krokinole, Lyonnesse, Madagascar, Nowhere, Olliphane, Pilgham, Quinine, Raratonga, Somewhere, Tantamount, Unicorn, Valisande, Walpurgis, Xion, Ys and Zacaranda—the names derived from legend, myth, romance, his own whimsey. One of the worlds was accompanied by a satellite, described in the dispatch as "an eccentric, tumbling, odd-shaped fragment of chondritic pumice," and this Roger Pilgham named "Sir Julian."

The press received and published the list and Rigel's planets became so known, though Sir Julian's acquaintances wondered about the sudden extravagance of his imagination. And who, or what, was "Pilgham"? Sir Julian presumably would explain upon his arrival.

The clerk, Roger Pilgham, presently returns to the obscurity from which he sprang, and there is no record of his conduct or state of mind as Sir Julian's return became imminent. Did he feel apprehension? Uneasiness? Indifference? Beyond all doubt he had become resigned to the prospect of discharge from his position.

In due course Sir Julian made a triumphant return, and in due course used the phrase, "most impressive perhaps are the New Grampian Mountains on the North Continent of Lord Bulwer-Lytton." A member of the audience politely asked the whereabouts of Lord Bulwer-Lytton, and the substitution was revealed.

Sir Julian's reaction to the deed was one of extraordinary fury. The clerk prudently went into seclusion; Sir Julian was encouraged to reintroduce his own nominations, but the damage had been done; Roger Pilgham's brash deed caught the fancy of the public, and Sir Julian's terminology gradually faded from memory.

From *Popular Handbook of the Planets,* 303rd Edition, published 1292:

Alphanor, a planet considered the administrative node and cultural center of the Rigel Concourse. It is eighth in orbital order.

Planetary Constants:

  Diameter 9300 miles

Mass	102
Mean Day	29 hours, 16 minutes,
etc.	29.4 seconds

General Remarks: Alphanor is a large bright sea world with a generally bracing climate. Ocean occupies three-quarters of the total surface, including the polar ice floes. The land mass is divided into seven nearly contiguous continents: Phrygia, Umbria, Lusitania, Scythia, Etruria, Lydia and Lycia, in a configuration suggesting seven petals of a flower. There are uncounted islands.

Autochthonous life is complex and vigorous. The flora has in no way yielded to terrestrial imports, which must be carefully tended and nurtured. The fauna is likewise complex, and on occasion actively savage; to cite the clever hyrcan major of upper Phrygia, and the invisible eel of the Thaumaturge Ocean.

The political structure of Alphanor is a pyramidal democracy—simple in theory, intricate in practice. The continents are divided into provinces, thence prefectures, districts and wards: these latter defined as population blocs of five thousand persons. Each ward committee sends a representative to the district council, which elects a delegate to the prefectural diet, which sends a member to the provincial congress, which does likewise for the continental parliament. Each parliament elects seven rectors to the Grand Council at Avente, in the Sea Province of Umbria, which thereupon chooses a chairman.

From Preface to *Peoples of the Concourse,* by Strick and Chernitz:

The Concourse populations are far from homogeneous. During the migrations from Earth racial groups tended to follow their own, and in the new environments, under the influence of interbreeding and new behavior patterns, such groups specialized even further.... The folk of Alphanor in general are fair, brown-haired, of medium stature, though an hour's walk along the Grand Esplanade at Avente will show the observer every conceivable style of human being.

The Alphanor psychology is more difficult to express. Every inhabited world is different in this regard; and though the differences are real and distinct

43

enough, it is hard to present them accurately without discursiveness—especially since each planetwide generalization is compounded, vitiated, or contradicted by regional differences.

* * * * * * *

Rigel, dead ahead, was a bright blue-white point from which every other star seemed to flee. Gersen had little to do but contemplate his destination, fight restlessness and tension, speculate regarding Attel Malagate's probable intentions, and formulate his own set of responses. The first problem: Where to land? One hundred and eighty-three spaceports on twenty-two of the twenty-six worlds were convenient to his lawful use, as well as unlimited desert and wasteland, should he choose to risk arrest for violation of the quarantine laws.

How intensely did Malagate want Teehalt's monitor? Would he arrange a watch at every spaceport? Theoretically, this could be done, by the suborning of port officials. The cheapest and perhaps most effective system would be to offer a resounding reward to the man who reported Gersen's arrival. Gersen of course might choose to set down at another star system. It would be difficult to mount guard over every space port of the Oikumene.

But it was by no means Gersen's purpose to go into hiding. In the next phase of proceedings he must necessarily expose himself. This next phase was the identification of Malagate. Two methods to this end suggested themselves: he could either trace the registry of the monitor, or await the approach of some member of Malagate's organization, and then try to trace the nerve of authority back to its source.

Malagate would take for granted Gersen's intent to investigate the monitor, and would presumably concentrate his vigilance at the Kindune spaceport, which served Sansontiana.

Nevertheless, for a series of indefinite reasons—little more than hunches—Gersen decided to land at the Grand Interplanetary Spaceport at Avente.

He approached Alphanor, coasted down into landing orbit, locked his autopilot into the official landing program, and once more sat back. The boat settled, bumped in a roar of expiring jets upon the scorched red earth. The jets died;

there was silence. Automatically the pressure-equalizing valve began to hiss.

The port officials approached in a slide car. Gersen anawered questions, submitted to a brief medical inspection, received an entry permit. The officials departed; a mobile crane trundled up, lifted the boat, carried it to a bay in the storage line at one side of the field.

Gersen descended to the ground, feeling exposed and vulnerable. He started to detach the monitor, keeping a careful lookout in all directions.

Two men sauntered along the storage line, casually, or so it seemed. Gersen recognized one of them instantly: the Sarcoy who had followed Hildemar Dasce into Smade's Tavern.

As they approached, Gersen gave them no overt heed, but they made no twitch or move that he did not observe. The Sarkoy wore a modest suit of dark gray with epaulettes embroidered with opals; his companion, a thin sandy-haired man with dancing white-gray eyes, wore a laborer's loose blue coverall.

The two stopped a few feet from Gersen, stood watching as if in casual interest. Gersen, after a glance, ignored them, though his skin crawled and his pulse pounded. The Sarkoy muttered something to his associate, came a little forward.

"I think we've met?" His voice was soft, sardonic.

"Your name evades me," said Gersen politely.

"I am Suthiro, Sivij Suthiro."

Gersen examined him carefully, seeing a man of middle weight, with the curious flat head of the Sarkoy Steppeman, * the face wider than high. Suthiro's eyes were soft dead olive-drab, the nose snub and dark of nostril, the mouth

*The Sarkoy were held in low esteem by other peoples of the Oïkumene, by virtue of repugnant eating habits and gross and exhibitionistic sexual conduct. Also despised was the popular Sarkoy sport known as *harbite*, or the baiting of a harikap, a large bristle-furred semi-intelligent biped of the north forests. The wretched creature, brought to a state of tension by hunger, would be thrust into a circle of men armed with pitchforks and torches, stimulated to wild activity by being set on fire, thrust deftly with pitchforks back ino the center of the circle as it sought to escape.

Sarkovy, the single planet of Phi Ophiuchi, was a dim world of steppes, swamps, black forests, morasses. The Sarkoy lived in tall wooden houses behind timber palisades; not even the largest of the towns was secure from the attack of bandits and nomads from the wastelands. By practice and tradition the Sarkoy were accomplished poisoners. A Master Venefice reportedly could kill a man merely by walking past him.

wide, thick-lipped—a face shaped by more than a thousand years of specialization and inbreeding. Gersen could not detect the "breath of death" an accomplishment forced upon indentured assassins, which shortened their lives, gave the skin a yellowish glaze, and caused the hair to stiffen. Suthiro's skin was untoned pallid ivory, his hair was a glossy black pelt, and he wore tattooed on his right cheek the small Maltese cross of the Sarkoy hetman.

Gersen said, "My apologies, Scop Suthiro. I don't remember the occasion you mention."

"Ah." Suthiro's eyes widened at Gersen's use of the honorific. "You have visited Sarkovy. Dear green Sarkovy, its boundless steppes, its merry festivals!"

"Merry, so long as the harikap last. Then what will you torture?"

Suthiro, of a race inured to insult, took no offense. "We always have each other. . . . I see you know my planet well."

"Fairly well. Perhaps you remember me from Sarkovy."

"No," said Suthiro wryly. "Elsewhere, and more recently."

Gersen shook his head. "Impossible. I have just come in from Beyond."

"Exactly. We met Beyond. At Smade's Tavern."

"Indeed."

"Yes. With certain others I came to meet my friend Lugo Teehalt. In the confusion and excitement Lugo left Smade's Planet in your spaceship. Surely you are aware of this?"

Gersen laughed. "If Teehalt has either apologies or complaints, I'm sure he will seek me out."

"Exactly," said Suthiro. "Lugo Teehalt sent me to make adjustment. He begs forgiveness for his mistake, and wishes only that I recover his monitor."

Gersen shook his head. "You can't have it."

"No?" Suthiro moved closer. "Lugo offers a thousand SVU* to indemnify you for his mistake."

"I accept with thanks. Give me the money."

"And the monitor?"

"I will return it when he comes for it."

The thin-faced man made an irritable clicking sound, but Suthiro grinned. "This is not exactly feasible. You will have the money, but we will not have the monitor."

"There is no reason why you should have the monitor. Lugo Teehalt is one principal in the matter; I will give

*SVU: Standard Value Unit of the Oikumene.

him his monitor. I am the other principal in the matter; it is perfectly legitimate for you to give me the money. Unless, of course, you distrust my honesty."

"By no means, since we do not intend to put it to the test. We propose, in fact, to take the monitor at this moment."

"I think not," said Gersen. "I plan to take possession of the filament."

"This is out of the question!" said Suthiro gently.

"Try to stop me." Gersen returned to work, disengaged the seals from the monitor housing.

Suthiro watched placidly. He made a signal to the thin-faced man, who backed away and kept lookout. "I could stop you so suddenly you'd become a marble statue." He looked over his shoulder to the thin-faced man, who nodded. Suthiro exhibited a weapon he carried in his hand. "I can provide you a heart spasm, a brain hemorrhage, or a convulsion of the small intestine, whichever you prefer."

Gersen paused in his work, drew a deep sigh. "Your arguments are impressive. Pay me five thousand SVU."

"I need pay you nothing. But here is the thousand I mentioned." He tossed Gersen a packet of notes, then motioned to the thin-faced man, who came forward, took Gersen's tools, and expertly detached the monitor. Gersen counted the money, moved to the side. The two dropped the monitor into a bag and, without another word, departed. Gersen laughed quietly. This was the monitor he had bought and installed at Euville, at a cost of four hundred SVU. Teehalt's monitor was safe inside the ship.

Gersen returned into the ship, closed the ports. Time now was of the essence. Suthiro would require about ten minutes to communicate his success, either to Dasce or conceivably to Malagate himself. Messages would then go out to various other spaceports of the Concourse, calling off the alert. Malagate would not receive the monitor, if Gersen were in luck, for several hours, perhaps not for days, depending upon his whereabouts. There would be an additional delay while the deception was discovered, and then Malagate's organization would once again be mobilized, the focus now upon the Feritse Precision Instrument Company at Sansontiana, on Olliphane.

By this time Gersen hoped to have been there and gone. Certainly he would have no time to spare. Without further delay he started the jets, rose into the blue Alphanor sky, pointed the boat toward Olliphane.

Chapter 5

From *Popular Handbook of the Planets:*

Olliphane, nineteenth planet of the Rigel Concourse.

Planetary Constants:

Diameter	6700 miles
Mass	0.9
etc.	

General Remarks: Olliphane is the most dense of the Rigel planets, and orbits close at the outer edge of the Habitable Zone. It has been speculated that when the proto-planet of the Third Group disintegrated Olliphane received an unduly large share of core materials. In any event, until recent astronomic times, Olliphane was subject to intense plutonic activity, and even today boasts ninety-two active volcanoes.

Olliphane is highly mineralized. An imposing relief provides vast hydro-electric potential, furnishing cheaper energy than is possible from traditional sources. A diligent disciplined population, utilizing these advantages, has made Olliphane the most highly industrialized world of the Concourse, rivaled only by Tantamount, with its shipyards, and Lyonnesse, with its monumental Gnome Iron Works.

Olliphane is relatively cool and wet, with the population concentrated in the Equatorial Zone, notably around the shores of Lake Clare. Here the visitor will find the ten largest cities of the planet, led by Kindune, Sansontiana, and New Ossining.

Olliphane is likewise nutritionally self-sufficient. Few other than natural foods are consumed, of which per capita consumption is highest in the Concourse, third highest among major worlds of the Oikumene. The alpine valleys surrounding the lake are devoted to dairying and the production of greenstuffs.

The Olphs are a mingled stock, derived primarily from a colony of Hyperborean Skakers. They are typically blond to brown of hair, large-boned, often inclined to corpulence, with fair undyed skins. They are respectful of orthodoxy, sedate in personal lives, but notoriously enthusiastic during the public fêtes and celebrations which serve as emotional release to an otherwise conventional and reserved folk.

A caste system, though without legal status, permeates every phase of the social structure. Prerogatives are carefully defined, jealously observed; the language has expanded and loosened to provide at least a dozen styles of address.

From "A Study of Inter-Class Accommodations," by Frerb Hankbert, in *Journal of the Anthropicene,* Vol. MCXIII:

It is a remarkable experience for a visitor to watch a pair of Olphs, strange to each other, appraising each other for caste. The operation requires no more than an instant, and appears almost intuitive, for the persons concerned may well be wearing standard garments.

I have questioned many Olphs in this matter, and can still make no definite assertions. In the first place most Olphs blandly deny the existence of caste structure, and consider their society completely egalitarian. In the second place, the Olphs themselves are not quite sure how they divine the caste of a stranger. He either has more of the quality known as *haute* than oneself, or less.

I have theorized that rapid unconscious and almost undetectable eye movements are the key to the assessment of *haute*, with characteristic shifts or steadiness indicative of each caste. Hands and hand motions may play a similar function.

As might be expected, high officials of the bureaucracy enjoy the most exalted caste, and especially the Civic Tutelars, as the Olphs name their police.

* * * * * * *

Gersen landed at the Kindune spaceport and, with Teehalt's monitor in a suitcase, boarded a subway for Sansontiana. To the best of his knowledge no one had heeded his arrival, no one had followed him.

But now time was growing short. At any moment Malagate must realize he had been duped and would seek to re-establish contact. For the moment Gersen considered himself safe; nevertheless, he performed a few classic maneuvers to disengage himself from stick-tight* or tracker. Finding nothing to disconcert him, he deposited the monitor in a public locker, at the subway interchange under the Rapunzel Hotel, retaining only the brass serial plate. Then, boarding an express car, he was delivered in fifteen minutes, to Sansontiana, eighty miles south. He consulted a directory, transferred to a local for the Ferristoun District, and presently was discharged into a station only a few hundred yards from the Feritse Precision Instrument Company.

Ferristoun was a dismal district of industrial structures, warehouses, an occasional tavern: these latter cheerful little nooks, lavish with ornament, colored glass, carved wood, in emulation of the grand pleasure arcades along the lake shore.

The time was middle morning; rain had darkened the black cobblestone pavement. Six-wheel drays lumbered along the streets, the entire district sounded to a subdued hum of engines. As Gersen walked a short sharp bleat of whistle signaled a change of shift; the sidewalks at once became crowded with workers. They were pale people, blank and humorless of face, wearing warm well-made coveralls in one of three colors: gray, dark blue, or mustard yellow; a contrasting belt, either black or white; black round-topped kaftans. All were standard issue, the government being an elaborate syndicalism, as thoroughgoing, careful and humorless as its constituency.

Two further bleats of the whistle sounded; as if by magic the streets cleared, the workers ducking into buildings like cockroaches exposed to the light.

A moment later Gersen came to a stained concrete façade on which large bronze letters read FERITSE, and below, in the hooked Olph script: *Precision Instruments*. Again

---

*Stick-tight—these come in at least five varieties, suitable to various applications:

    The servo-optical—a spy cell supported on rotary wings, remotely guided by an operator.

    The automatic—a similar cell to follow a radioactive or monochromatic tag fixed to, or smeared upon, a man or vehicle.

    The Culp spy master—a semi-intelligent flying creature trained to follow any subject of interest; clever, cooperative, reliable, but relatively large and noticeable.

    The Manx spy bird—a smaller, less obtrusive creature, trained to perform similarly; less docile and intelligent, more aggressive.

    The Manx spy bird modification—similar to the above, equipped with control devices.

50

it had become necessary to expose himself to his enemies; the prospect was far from comfortable. Well, there was no help for it. A single small door led into the building. Gersen entered, to find himself in a long dim hallway, a concrete tunnel, which after a hundred feet brought him to the administration offices. He went to stand at a counter, and was approached by an elderly woman of pleasant appearance and manner. By local custom, she wore masculine garments while at work; a dark blue suit with a black belt. Recognizing Gersen as an off-worlder, of unguessable caste, she bowed with unctuous courtesy and asked in a low reverent voice: "How, sir, may we serve you?"

Gersen tendered the brass plate. "I have lost the key to my monitor, and I want a duplicate."

The woman blinked. Her manner underwent an instant, if unconscious, change. She reached hesitantly for the plate, held it between thumb and forefinger as if it were tainted, looked over her shoulder.

"Well?" asked Gersen in a voice made suddenly harsh by tension. "Is there any difficulty?"

"There are new regulations," the woman muttered. "I have had instructions to.... I must consult Director-controller Masensen. Excuse me, sir."

She went almost at a trot to a side door, disappeared. Gersen waited, the subconscious perceptors in his brain ticking and prickling. He was more nervous than he cared to be; nervousness clouded the judgment, affected the accuracy of observation.... The woman slowly returned to the counter, looking to right and left, evading Gersen's eyes. "Just a moment, sir. If you will wait.... There are records to be inspected; isn't this the way always? When a person wishes haste...."

"Where is the serial plate?" asked Gersen.

"Director-Controller Masensen has taken it into charge."

"In that case, I'll speak to Director-Controller Masensen at once."

"I will inquire," said the woman.

"Please don't bother," said Gersen. Ignoring her startled squeak of protest, he let himself through a swinging door, passed ahead of her into the inner chamber. A portly thick-faced man in faddish Special Issue blue and dove gray sat at a desk talking into a telephone. He looked at the brass serial plate as he spoke. At the sight of Gersen his eyebrows rose, his mouth sagged in irritation and dismay. Quickly he laid down the telephone. There was an instant while his eyes flicked up and down Gersen's clothes before he shouted, "Who are you, sir? Why do you come into my room?"

Gersen reached across the desk, took possession of the serial plate. "Who do you telephone in connection with this matter?"

Masensen became fiercely haughty. "None of your concern, whatsoever! Impudence! Here in my office!"

Gersen spoke in a soft even voice. "The Tutelars will be interested in your illegal actions. I am puzzled that you choose to defy the law."

Masensen sat back, in puff-cheeked alarm. The Tutelars, of a caste so elevated that the distinction between Masensen and his office clerk would seem insignificant, were not to be trifled with. They were no respecters of persons; they tended to believe the accusation rather than the protestation of innocence. They wore uniforms of a sumptuous thick pile which showed various sheens according to the light: plum, dark green, gold. Not so much arrogant as intensely serious, they conducted themselves to the full implications of their caste. On Olliphane penal torture was administered as a cheaper, if not more effective, deterrent than fines of imprisonment; the threat of a police accusation could therefore bring consternation to the most innocent.

Director-Controller Masensen cried out, "I have never defied the law! Do I refuse your request? No indeed."

"Then furnish my key immediately, as the law requires."

"Softly then," said Masensen. "We cannot go so fast. There are records to inspect. Don't forget, we have more important affairs than leaping to serve every raggle-taggle vagabond of a locater who marches into our room to insult us."

Gersen stared into the round pale face, which gave back hostility and defiance. "Very well," said Gersen. "I will go to complain before the Board of Tutelars."

"Now then, be reasonable!" blurted Masensen in heavy affability. "All things do not come at once."

"Where is my key? Do you still plan to defy the law?"

"Naturally, no such thing is possible. I will see to the matter. Come, be patient. Take a chair and compose yourself for just these few minutes."

"I do not care to wait."

"Go, then!" bellowed Masensen. "I have done exactly as the law requires!" His lips were pushing in and out; his face was pink with fury; he hammered the desk with his fists. The clerk, standing horrified in the doorway, emitted a low wail of terror. "Bring the Tutelars!" raged Masensen. "I will accuse you of molestation and threats! I will see you whipped!"

Gersen dared delay no longer. Furiously he turned, departed. He passed through the outer office and out into the concrete tunnel. He paused, turned a quick look behind him. The receptionist, fluttering in excitement, paid him no heed. Grinning like a wolf, Gersen walked up the hall, away from the entrance, and presently came to an arched opening giving upon the production chambers.

Standing to the side, inconspicuous in the shadow of a pilaster, he made a careful appraisal of the rooms, tracing the various production lines. Certain phases were under biomechanical control, others were performed by debtors, moral deviants, vagrants or drunks, leased by the dozen from the city. They sat chained to their benches, guarded by an old warden, and worked with apathetic efficiency. The room supervisor sat on an elevated platform, which could swing on a boom to any area of the room.

Gersen located the process where monitors were constructed, identified the area where locks were installed: an alcove two hundred feet along the wall, beside a cubicle where a clerical worker, perhaps a timekeeper, sat on a high chair.

He made a final survey of the room. No one had showed the slightest interest in him. The supervisor's attention was turned elsewhere. He walked quickly along the wall to the cubicle where the clerk sat: a harassed hollow-cheeked young-old man, with sardonic black eyebrows, a wrinkled sallow skin, a cynical hook of nose and curl of mouth: a man not necessarily a pessimist, but apparently one without optimism. Gersen stepped to the back of the cubicle, where there were shadows.

The clerk looked around in astonishment. "Well, sir? What do you wish? This is not permitted; you must know that."

Gersen asked, "Would you care to earn a hundred SVU —very quickly?"

The clerk grimaced sadly. "Of course. Who must I kill?"

"My wants are less demanding," said Gersen. He displayed the brass plate. "Get me the key for this instrument, and fifty SVU is yours." He placed five purple notes on the table. "Find out to whom the serial number is registered—fifty SVU more." He counted down the notes.

The clerk looked at the money, then turned a speculative glance over his shoulder, out across the shop. "Why not go to the front office? The Director-Controller usually handles such things."

"I have irritated Director-Controller Masensen," said Gersen. "He makes difficulties, and I am in a hurry."

"In other words, Director-Controller Masensen would not approve of my helping you."

"Which is why I offer you the hundred SVU to perform an entirely legal errand for me."

"Is it worth my job?"

"If I leave by the back way, no one need know. And Masensen will never know the difference."

The clerk considered. "Very well," he said. "I can do it. But I'll need another fifty SVU for the keymaker."

Gersen shrugged, brought forth an orange fifty SVU note. "I will appreciate haste."

The clerk laughed. "From my viewpoint, the sooner you are gone the better. I'll have to look through two sets of records. We're not too efficient here. Meanwhile keep to the back, out of sight." He noted the serial number, left the cubicle, disappeared behind a partition.

Time passed. Gersen noticed that the back wall was paneled with painted glass. Bending, he put his eye to a scratch and obtained a blurred view of the room behind the partition.

The clerk stood at an old-fashioned filing case, flipping cards. He found the file, made a set of notes. But now from a side door Masensen lumbered into the room. The clerk closed the file, walked away. Masensen stopped short, fired a question at the clerk, who responded with an indifferent word or two. Gersen paid silent tribute to his *sang-froid*. Masensen glared after him, then wheeled and went to the files.

With one eye on Masensen's burly back, the clerk bent over the keymaker, whispered in his ear, departed. Masensen looked around suspiciously, but the clerk had left the room.

The machinist dropped a key blank into the machine, consulted a paper, punched a set of buttons to control the notches, twists, conductivities and magnetic nodes of the key.

Masensen rummaged through the files, extracted a card, marched from the room. The clerk at once returned. The machinist tossed him the key; the clerk came back to the cubicle. He handed the key to Gersen, took five purple notes from the table.

"And the registration?" asked Gersen.

"I can't help you. Masensen got to the files ahead of me and removed the card."

Gersen glumly considered the key. His main purpose had been to learn the registered owner of the monitor. The key of course was better than nothing; the record filament was easier to hide than the monitor itself. But time was short; he dared delay no longer. "Keep the other fifty," he said. The money, after all, had come from Malagate. "Buy your children a present."

The clerk shook his head. "I accept pay only for what I achieve. I need no gift."

"As you wish." Gersen returned the money to his pocket. "Tell me how to leave inconspicuously."

"You had better go the way you came," said the clerk. "If you try to go out the back way you will be stopped by the patrol."

"Thank you," said Gersen. "You are not Olph?"

"No. But I've lived here so long I've forgotten anything better."

Gersen looked cautiously from the cubicle. The situation was as before. He slipped out, walked quickly along the wall to the arch, slipped through into the concrete tunnel. Passing the door which led into the administration offices, he looked through, saw Masensen pacing back and forth, evidently in a vicious mood. Gersen stepped past, hurried down the hall toward the outside door.

But now this door opened. A man entered, his features dark against the outside light. Gersen continued forward briskly, confidently, as if his business were the most legitimate in the world.

The man approached; their eyes met. The newcomer stopped: it was Tristano the Earthman.

"Luck!" declared Tristano in a voice of hushed pleasure. "Luck indeed."

Gersen made no reply. Slowly, carefully, he sought to sidle past, too nervous and tense to feel fear. Tristano took a step, blocked his way. Gersen halted, appraised him. Tristano was shorter than himself by an inch, but thick in the neck and shoulders, flat but rather wide at the hips: an attribute indicating agility and good muscular leverage. His head was small, almost hairless; his features were neat. The ears were surgically cropped, the nose flat, the area around the mouth thick with muscle. His expression was calm, with a serene secret half-smile twisting up the corners of his mouth. He seemed reckless rather than vicious: a man who would feel neither hate nor pity, a man driven only by the need to fulfill the extremes of his capabilities. A highly dangerous man, thought Gersen. He said quietly, "Stand aside."

Tristano extended his left hand almost affably. "Whatever your name is, be wise. Come with me." Flicking and weaving the extended hand, he leaned forward. Gersen watched Tristano's eyes, ignoring the distracting left hand. When the right hand darted forth he knocked it aside, drove his fist into Tristano's face.

Tristano reeled back, as if in desperate pain, and Gersen pretended to be deceived. He rushed forward, arm cocked back to administer another blow, then halted abruptly as with incredible agility Tristano swung up his leg: a kick intended to cripple or kill. As the foot swung by, Gersen seized toe and heel, twisted hard. Tristano, relaxing instantly, turned in mid-air, pulled himself into a ball, used the momentum of his turn and fall to wrench the foot harmlessly from Gersen's grasp. He caught himself catlike on hands and feet, started to bounce away, but Gersen caught the back of Tristano's head, yanked Tristano's face down against his knee. Cartilege crushed, teeth broke.

Tristano fell back, now startled. For an instant he sat laxly asprawl. Gersen caught Tristano's leg and ankle in a lock, threw over his weight, and felt the bone snap. Tristano sucked in his breath. Snatching for his knife, he left his throat exposed; Gersen hacked backhand at the larynx. Tristano's throat was well-muscled, and he retained consciousness, but fell back, feebly waving his knife. Gersen kicked it away, but edged forward carefully, for Tristano might be equipped with one or a dozen secret built-in weapons.

"Leave me be," croaked Tristano. "Leave me be, go your way." He dragged himself to the wall.

Gersen cautiously reached forth, giving Tristano the option to counter. Tristano refused; Gersen made contact with the massive shoulders, gripped. Tristano suffered this. The two stared eye to eye. Tristano made a sudden grab for an armlock, simultaneously bringing up his good leg. Gersen avoided the armlock, seized the leg, prepared to break the other ankle. Behind him there was outcry, a flurry of movement. Director-Controller Masensen, face contorted, came running awkwardly down the hall. Behind him trotted two or three underlings.

"Stop this!" cried Masensen. "What do you do here, in this building?" He fairly spat in Gersen's face, "You are a devil, a criminal of the worst sort! You insult me, you attack my customer! I will have the Tutelars attend to you!"

"By all means," panted Gersen, suddenly brimming with vindictiveness. "Call the Tutelars."

Masensen raised his eyebrows. "What? You have this insolence too?"

"No insolence is intended," said Gersen. "A good citizen assists the police in apprehending criminals."

"What do you mean?"

"There is a certain name which I need speak only once to the Tutelars. I need only hint that you and this person are in collusion. For proof? This man—" he looked down at the half-smiling, half-dazed Tristano—"do you know him?"

"No. Of course I do not know him."

"But you identified him as a customer."

"So I thought him."

"He is a notorious murderer."

"Wrong, my agile friend," croaked Tristano. "No murderer I."

"Lugo Teehalt is not alive to contradict you."

Tristano essayed a grimace of outraged innocence. "We spoke, you and I, while the old man died."

"In this case, neither Dasce nor the Sarkoy killed Teehalt. Who came with you to Smade's Planet?"

"We came alone."

Gersen stared in puzzlement. "I find this hard to believe. Hildemar Dasce told Teehalt that Malagate awaited him outside."

Tristano's response was a faint shrug.

Gersen stood looking down at him. "I respect the Tutelars and their scourges; I dare not kill you. But I can break more bones, and you will walk sideways like a crab. I can spread apart your eyes, and you will look in two different directions the rest of your life."

The lines bracketing Tristano's mouth became deep and melancholy. He slumped heavily back against the wall, uninterested, sodden with pain. He mumbled, "Since when is killing beyond the Pale called murder?"

"Who killed Teehalt?"

"I saw nothing. I stood with you, by the door."

"But the three of you came together to Smade's."

Tristano made no response. Gersen leaned forward, performed a quick vicious act. Masensen made an inarticulate sound, stumbled away; then, halting as if caught by a wire, he slowly turned to stare. Tristano looked numbly at his dangling hand.

"Who killed Teehalt?"

Tristano shook his head. "I will say no more. I would rather limp and squint than die of the Sarkoy's cluthe."

"I can infect you with cluthe."

"I will say no more."

Gersen leaned forward, but Masensen uttered a short quavering cry. "This is intolerable! I will not allow it! Must you give me nightmares? I do not sleep well."

Gersen examined him without friendliness. "You would do well not to interfere."

"I will call in the Tutelars. Your acts are grossly illegal; you have broken laws of the state."

Gersen laughed. "Call the Tutelars. We will learn who has broken laws and who will be punished."

Masensen rubbed his pallid cheeks. "Go then. Never return, and I will say no more."

"Not so fast," said Gersen, in high good spirits. "You are in serious difficulties. I came here on a legal errand; you telephone for a murderer, who attacks me. This conduct no one should ignore."

Masensen licked his lips. "You are making false charges; I will add this to my particulars." It was a poor effort. Gersen laughed. He went to Tristano, turned him over on his face, pulled the jacket down the broad back to constrict the arms, tied it in place with Tristano's sash. With his broken bones Tristano was now immobilized.

Gersen stepped down the hall, motioned to Masensen. "Let us go to your office."

Gersen led the way, with Masensen stumping reluctantly behind; once within the inner office, Masensen sank on nerveless legs into his chair.

"Now then," said Gersen, "call the Tutelars."

Masensen shook his head. "It—it is better to make no difficulties. The Tutelars are sometimes unreasonable."

"In that case you must tell me what I want to know."

Masensen bowed his head. "Ask."

"Who did you telephone when I appeared?"

Masensen showed extreme agitation. "I cannot tell you," he said huskily. "Do you insist that I be killed?"

"The Tutelars will ask the same question, as well as many others."

Masensen looked in anguish to right, left, up at the ceiling.

58

"A man," he said, "at the Grand Pomador Hotel. His name
—Spock."

"I know better," said Gersen. "You are lying. I give you
one more chance. Who did you call?"

Masensen shook his head desperately. "I do not lie."

"Have you seen the man?"

"Yes. He is tall. He has short pink hair, a long big head
and no neck. His face is a peculiar red color, and he wears
dark spectacles, and a nose guard—very unusual. He has no
more feeling than a fish."

Gersen nodded. Masensen was telling the truth. This would
be Hildemar Dasce. He turned. "Now then, this is most important. I wish to know to whom the monitor is registered."

Masensen started to shake his head, then gave a fatalistic
shrug and rose to his feet. "I will go for the record."

"No," said Gersen. "We will go together. And if we cannot
find the record, I swear to you I will lodge the strongest
possible charges."

Masensen rubbed his forehead wearily. "I remember now.
The record is here." He brought forth a card from his desk.
"Sea Province University, Avente, Alphanor. Beneficial Grant
291."

"No name?"

"No. And there is no value to you in the key. The university uses a coder in each of its monitors. We have sold them
several."

"Indeed." The use of a coder, to thwart the double-dealing
of an unscrupulous locater, was common enough.

Masensen's voice became heavily ironic. "The university
has evidently sold you a coded monitor without the descrambling strip. If I were you I would complain to the Avente
authorities."

Gersen considered the implications of the information. They
were far-reaching indeed, if one certain condition were met.

"Why did you telephone the man Spock? Did he offer you
money?"

Masensen nodded miserably. "Money. And—he made
threats. An indiscretion in my past—" he made a vague gesture.

"Tell me, did Spock realize that the monitor was coded?"

"Certainly. I mentioned this to him, but he was already
aware of it."

Gersen nodded. The condition had been met. Attel Malagate must necessarily have access to the descrambling strip at
the Sea Province University.

He reflected for a moment. Information was accumulating. Malagate himself had killed Teehalt, if Hildemar Dasce were to be believed. Tristano indirectly had verified this; he had conveyed more information than he meant to. He had also confused the situation. If Dasce, the Sarkoy poisoner, and Tristano had come together, with no fourth person, how was the presence of Malagate to be explained? Had he arrived simultaneously in another ship? Possible, but unlikely. . . .

Masensen was staring at him anxiously, miserably.

"I'm going now," said Gersen. "Do you plan to tell this Spock that I was here?"

Masensen nodded, all his bluster departed. "I must."

"But you will wait one hour."

Masensen made no protest. He might or might not respect Gersen's wishes—most likely not. But there was no help for this. Gersen turned, departed the office, leaving Masensen utterly deflated.

Walking down the hall Gersen overtook Tristano, who somehow had managed to squirm and writhe himself erect. Now he hopped down the hall, one foot dragging at a queer angle. He looked over his shoulder at Gersen, still wearing the quiet half smile, though the muscles around his mouth were tight. Gersen stopped to consider the man. It would be wise and desirable to kill him, except for the possibility of police interference. So, contenting himself with a polite nod, and stepping past Tristano, he went his way.

Chapter 6

Preface to *Men of the Oikumene,*
by Jan Holberk Vaenz LXII:

There is a stifling quality to this age which has been observed, remarked on and lamented by a number of the contemporary anthropologists: an oddity, for never before have such variegated opportunities and possible channels of life existed. It is profitable to consider this situation, for it will recur many times in the pages to follow.

The most important fact of human life is the infinity of space: the bounds which can never be reached, the worlds without number still unseen—in short, the Beyond. It is my belief that the awareness of these awesome possibilities has somehow clotted at the core of human consciousness, and has diminished or dampened human enterprise.

An instant qualification is necessary. Men of enterprise indeed exist, though sadly enough most of them work Beyond, and their enterprise is not entirely constructive. (The statement is not completely ironical: many of the most noxious forms of life exert some sort of useful side effect.)

But, in general, ambition is turned inward, rather than out toward the obvious goals. Why? Does infinity, as an object of experience instead of a mathematical abstraction, daunt the human mind? Are we complacent and secure, knowing that the riches of the galaxy are always there for the taking? Is contemporary life already sated by too rich a diet of novelty? Is it conceivable that the Institute wields more control over the human psyche than we suspect? Or is there current a feeling of frustration and staleness, the conviction that all glory has been won, that all the meaningful goals have been achieved?

Undoubtedly there is no single answer. But several points are noteworthy. First (to be mentioned without comment) is the peculiar situation where the most influential and effective systems of the day are the private, or at best semipublic, associations: the IPCC, the Institute, the Jarnell Corporation.

Second is the decline of the general level of education. The extremes are certainly farther apart; the savants of the Institute on the one hand, and, say, the serfs of a Tertullian estate on the other. If we consider the condition of men beyond the Pale, the polarity is even more pronounced. There are obvious sources to the decline. Pioneers settling in strange and often hostile environments have sheer survival for their first concern. Possibly even more daunting is the unmanageable mass of accumulated knowledge. The trend toward specialization began with modern times, but after the breakout into space, and the consequent new amplitude of information, specialization has become even more narrowly focused.

It is perhaps pertinent to consider the manner of man who has become the new specialist. He lives in a materialistic age, where comparatively small interest is given to absolutes. He is a man of charm, wit, sophistication, but no profundity. His ideals are not abstract. His field of endeavor, if he is a scholar, may be mathematics or one of the physical sciences; but it is a hundred times more likely to be a phase

61

of what loosely are called humanistic studies: history, sociology, comparatives, symbology, esthetics, anthropology, the varieties of experience, penology, education, communication, administration and coercion, not to mention the morass of psychology already trampled by generations of incompetents, and the still unexplored wilderness of psionics.

There are also those who, like the author, ensconce themselves on a thunderous crag of omniscience, and with protestations of humility which are either unconvincing or totally absent, assume the obligation of appraisal, commendation, derogation or denunciation of their contemporaries. Still, by and large it is an easier job than digging a ditch.

From *Ten Explorers: A Study of a Type*,
by Oscar Anderson:

Every world has its distinctive psychic aroma: this is a matter attested to by each of the ten explorers. Isack Canaday is willing to wager that if he were blindfolded and taken to any planet of the Oikumene or the immediate Beyond, he would correctly identify this planet immediately upon removal of the blindfold. How does he perform such a feat? At first glance it seems incomprehensible. Canaday himself professes not to know the source of his knowledge. "I just raise my nose, I look around the sky, I take a couple jumps—and it comes to me."

Canaday's explanation is of course arch and consciously quaint. Our senses are undoubtedly much more acute than we suspect. The composition of the air, the color of the light and the sky, the curvature and proximity of the horizon, the tension of gravity: these are presumably interpreted in our brains to produce an individuality, exactly as the sight of eyes, a nose, hair, a mouth, ears, creates the look of a face.

All of this without mention of flora and fauna, the artifices of autochthone or man, the possibly distinctive look of sun or suns. . . .

From *Life,* Volume III,
by Unspiek, Baron Bodissey:

As a society matures, the struggle for survival imperceptibly graduates and changes emphasis, and becomes what can only be termed the quest for pleasure. This is a large statement, possibly of no startling novelty. Nevertheless, as a generality, it affords a rich resonance of implications. The author suggests as a lively topic for a dissertation a survey of various environment-survival situations and the special types of pleasure goals deriving therefrom. It seems probable, from a moment's reflection, that every particular scarcity or compulsion or danger generates a corresponding psychic tension demanding a particular gratification.

*   *   *   *   *   *   *

Gersen returned to the subway terminal at Sansontiana. He recovered the monitor, immediately made a trial of the key. To his gratification the lock moved smoothly, the case slid open.

There was neither explosive nor acid present. He extracted the little cylinder containing the filament, weighed it in his hand. Then he stepped into a post-office booth and mailed the cylinder to himself at the Hotel Credenza, Avente, Alphanor. He rode the subway back to Kindune and the spaceport, and with no untoward incident took his ship aloft.

The blue crescent of Alphanor presently bulged across the sky, with Rigel dazzling beyond. When the seven continents began to emerge from the dark, Gersen engaged his autopilot into the Avente landing program, and so was guided down to the spaceport. The crane lifted the boat, carried it to a storage bay; Gersen emerged, made a cautious reconnaissance. Finding no evidence of his enemies, he proceeded down the ranks of stored spacecraft to the terminal building. Here he breakfasted and considered his plans. They were, he decided, completely straightforward, deriving from a progression of logical steps in which he could see no flaw:

a. Lugo Teehalt's monitor was registered to the Sea Province University.

b. The information on the monitor filament was coded, accessible only upon application of the decoding, or descrambling, strip.

c. The decoding strip was in possession of the Sea Province University at Avente.

d.

   1. According to Lugo Teehalt, Attel Malagate had been his original sponsor (a fact he had apparently understood for the first time at Brinktown. Indiscretions by Hildemar Dasce? Everything considered, Malagate probably still regarded his incognito secure).

   2. Malagate vigorously sought possession of the monitor

63

and its filament, and hence must have access to the decoding strip.

  e. Gersen's course of action would therefore be:

    1. Identify the persons who had access to the decoding strip.

    2. Learn which of these fulfilled a set of conditions consistent with the identity and activities of Malagate. Which, for example, had been gone long enough for a visit to Smade's Planet?

A straightforward and logical line of attack indeed. But, Gersen reflected, the implementation of his logic might not be quite so easy. He dare not arouse Malagate's apprehensions. To a certain extent, possession of Teehalt's filament provided security; however, if Malagate felt a personal threat, he would find little difficulty, and no qualms, in arranging an assassination. To this moment, Malagate had no reason to fear exposure, and it would be foolhardy to convince him otherwise. The initiative, for the present, was Gersen's; there was no occasion for breakneck haste. . . . His attention became distracted. In a booth nearby sat a pair of pretty girls who evidently had come to the terminal to welcome a friend, or to see one off. Gersen contemplated them wistfully, aware, not for the first time, of an empty area in his life, and feeling a dissatisfaction not unlike the indefinable emotion he had known at Smade's Planet. Frivolity . . . the two girls evidently had very little else on their minds. One had dyed her hair forest green and toned her skin a delicate lettuce green. The other wore a wig of lavender metal shavings with dead-white skin toning; an elaborate cloche of silver leaves and tendrils clung to her forehead, clasped her cheeks.

Gersen drew a deep breath. Undoubtedly he had lived a grim, cheerless existence. Thinking back across the years, scenes came crowding into his mind, all of which were variations on a single theme: other children occupied with irresponsible pleasure, while he, a rather thin boy with a grave face, watched from a distance. He had felt only interest and wonder at the easy gaiety—so he recalled—never relating the scenes to himself. His grandfather had seen to that. . . .

One of the girls at the nearby booth had noticed his attention; she whispered to her friend. Both glanced across the aisle, then ostentatiously ignored him. Gersen smiled ruefully. He felt no confidence in his dealings with women; he had known few intimately. He frowned, turned the two a wary side glance. Not impossibly, Malagate had sent these girls to beguile him. Ridiculous. Why two? They rose and departed the restaurant, each turning on him one swift covert glance.

Gersen watched their retreat, resisting the sudden urge to run after them, to introduce himself, to make them his friends. . . . Ridiculous again, doubly ridiculous. What would he say? He pictured the two pretty faces at first puzzled, then embarrassed, while he stood making lame efforts to ingratiate himself. The girls were gone. Just as well, thought Gersen, half amused, half angry with himself. Still, why deceive himself? Living the life of half a man was difficult, a source of dissatisfaction. The circumstances of his life had given him small command of the social graces.

Still, what of that? He knew his mission in life, and he was superbly prepared to fulfill this mission. He had no doubts, no uncertainties; his goals were exactly defined. A sudden idea disturbed the flow of his self-reassurances: Where would he be without this clear purpose? If he were less artificially motivated, he might not show so well in comparison with the easy men around him, with their pleasant manners and fluent talk. . . . Turning the thought over, back and forth, Gersen began to feel spiritually deficient. No phase of his life had occurred by his own free choice. He felt no slightest tremor in his dedication: this was not the point at issue. But, he thought, a man's goals should not be imposed upon him until he knew enough of the world to make his own survey, to weigh his own decisions. He had not been given this option. The decision had been made, he had accepted it. . . . After all, what matter? More to the point, what would he do when and if he succeeded in his aims? The chances were small, of course. But—assuming the death of five men—what then would he do with his life? Once or twice before he had reached this point in his reflections; warned by some subconscious signal, he had never gone beyond it. Nor did he do so now. His breakfast was finished; the girls, who had prompted him to his brooding, had taken themselves off. Evidently they were not agents of Malagate the Woe.

Gersen sat a few minutes longer considering the best approach to his problem, and again decided upon simple directness.

He went to a communication booth and was connected to the Information Bureau at the Sea Province University in the suburb of Remo, ten miles south.

The telescreen flickered first with the university seal, then a conventional reception presentation, printed with the words,

Please speak clearly. Simultaneously a recorded voice asked, "How may we serve you?"

Gersen spoke to the still unseen receptionist. "I want information regarding the university's exploration program. Which department is directly concerned?"

The screen clarified through a decorative cross-hatching to show the gold-toned face of a young woman with blonde hair in flamboyant puffs at each ear. "That depends on the type of exploration."

"It would be connected with Beneficial Grant 291."

"Just a moment, sir, and I'll inquire." The scene retreated behind the cross-hatching.

Presently the girl's face reappeared. "I'll connect you with the Department of Galactic Morphology, sir."

Gersen looked into another pale receptionist face. This young woman had arch piquant features toned nacreous silver, and wore her hair in a dark nimbus of ten thousand tiny varnished spikes. "Galactic Morph."

"I want to inquire about Beneficial Grant 291," said Gersen.

The girl considered for a moment. "You mean the grant itself, sir?"

"The grant, how it operates, who administers it."

The arch young face pursed its mouth dubiously. "There's not much I can tell you, sir. It's the fund which finances our exploration program."

"I'm particularly interested in a locater named Lugo Teehalt, who worked under the grant."

She shook her head. "I wouldn't know anything about him. Mr. Detteras could tell you, but he's not available for appointments today."

"Mr. Detteras hires the locaters?"

The girl twisted her eyebrows, squinted; she had a mobile expression, a wide mouth with a merry upward twitch at the corners. Gersen watched her in fascination. "I don't know too much about things like that, sir. We have our part in the Master Exploration Program, of course. That's not under Grant 291, though. Mr. Detteras is Director of Exploration; he could tell you whatever you wanted to know.

"Is there anyone else in the department who might sponsor a locater on Grant 291?"

The girl looked speculatively sidewise at Gersen, wondering as to the nature of his interest. "Are you a police official?" she asked timidly.

Gersen laughed. "No, I'm a friend of Mr. Teehalt's, trying to finish up some business for him."

"Oh. Well, there's Mr. Kelle who is Chairman of the Research Planning Committee. And Mr. Warweave, the Honorary Provost, who made the donation for Grant 291. Mr. Kelle is gone for the morning; his daughter is marrying tomorrow and he's very busy."

"What about Mr. Warweave? Can I see him?"

"Well—" the girl pursed her lips, bent her head over an appointment panel. "He's busy until three, and then he keeps an open hour, for students or persons without appointments."

"That would suit me very well."

"If you'd care to leave your name," said the girl demurely, "I'll put it at the head of the list. Then you won't have to wait, in case there are lots of others."

Gersen was startled by her solicitude. He searched her face, and was further surprised to find her smiling at him. "That's very kind of you, "My name is Kirth Gersen."

He watched her write. She seemed in no hurry to terminate the conversation. He asked, "What does an Honorary Provost do? What are his duties?"

She shrugged. "I don't know, really. He comes and goes. I think he does just what he wants. Anyone who is rich does just what he wants. Wait till I'm rich."

"One more thing," Gersen said. "Are you familiar with the routine of the department?"

"Why yes, I should say so." The girl laughed. "In so far as there is a routine."

"The recording lament of the monitor in a locater boat is coded. You're aware of this?"

"So I have been told." The girl was definitely speaking to Gersen as an individual, rather than a face on a screen. Gersen thought her deliciously pretty, in spite of her rather extravagant hair style. Definitely he had been in space too long. He kept his voice even with an effort. "Who unscrambles the filaments? Who is in charge of the code?"

Again the girl was doubtful. "Mr. Detteras for one. Perhaps Mr. Kelle."

"Can you find out definitely?"

The girl hesitated, examining Gersen's face. It was always wise to refuse to answer questions whose motives she could not fathom; still—where could be the harm? The man who inquired seemed interesting: wistful and sad, so she thought, and a trifle mysterious; and definitely not unattractive, in a hardbitten fashion. "I can ask Mr. Detteras' secretary," she said brightly. "Will you wait?"

The screen dimmed, and a minute or two later brightened

again. The girl smiled back at Gersen. "I was right. Mr Detteras, Mr. Kelle, and Mr. Warweave—these are the only people who have access to the decoding strip."

"I see. Mr. Detteras is Director of Exploration, Mr. Kelle is Chairman of the Research Planning Committee, and Mr. Warweave is—what?"

"Honorary Provost. They gave him the title when he endowed the department with Grant 291. He's a very wealthy man, and very interested in space exploration. He frequently goes Beyond. . . . Have you ever been Beyond?"

"I've just returned."

She leaned forward, her face alive with interest. "Is it really as wild and dangerous as everyone says?"

Gersen threw caution to the winds, with a bravado that startled even himself. "Come out with me and see for yourself."

The girl did not appear unduly perturbed. But she shook her head. "I'd be alarmed. I've been taught never to trust strange men from the Beyond. You might be a slaver and sell me."

"Such things have happened," said Gersen dampened. "You're probably safer where you are."

"Still," she said coquettishly, "who wants to be safe?"

Gersen hesitated, started to speak, stopped short. The girl watched him with an expression of bland innocence. Well, why not? he asked himself. His grandfather had been old and parched. . . .

"In that case—if you're willing to risk it—perhaps you'd spend the evening with me."

"For what purpose?" The girl was suddenly demure. "Slavery?"

"No. Just—the usual. Whatever you'd like to do."

"This is very abrupt. After all, I haven't even seen you face to face."

"Yes, you're right," said Gersen once more abashed. "I'm not very gallant."

"And still, what could be the harm? I'm impulsive myself, or so I've been told."

"I suppose it depends on circumstances."

"You're just in from Beyond," the girl said magnanimously. "So I guess you can be excused."

"Then you'll do it?"

She pretended to consider. "Very well. I'll take a chance. Where will I meet you?"

"I'll be out at three o'clock to see Mr. Warweave; we can make arrangements then."

"I'm off duty at four.... You're sure you're not a slaver?"

"I'm not even a pirate."

"Rather an unenterprising sort, I'd say.... But I'm just as pleased, until I know you a little better."

* * * * * * *

A wide sandy beach extended a hundred miles south of Avente, around the entire concavity of Ard Hook. As far as Remo, and a few miles beyond, villas built of glaring white coquina lined the crest of the sandy bluffs which overlooked the ocean.

Gersen hired a car, a small surface slider, and skidded south over the broad white turnpike, the inevitable dust puffing up behind him. For a space the road followed the shore. Sand dazzled under the brilliant Rigel light; blue water under a collar of white foam sparkled and rolled calmly up and down the sand, creating a sound invariable on every world in every galaxy where surf meets shore. The road presently climbed the bluffs; to the left spread sand dunes overgrown with black and purple iron bush, punctuated by tall white balloon flower, the inflated pod floating at the end of a long stem. Other white villas looked forth from groves of cool green deodars, native feathertree, hybrid palm.

Ahead the ground rose, and the sandy bluffs became a range of low hills, presenting a steep face to the ocean. Remo occupied the flat land at the foot of one of these hills. A pair of piers terminating in high-domed casinos reached forth to create a harbor filled with small boats. The university occupied the crest of the hill: a series of low, flat-roofed structures connected by arcades.

Gersen arrived at the campus parking area, lowered the slide car, alighted. A slideway took him through a commemorative arch into a wide mall, where he inquired directions from a student.

"The College of Galactic Morphology? Into the next quad, sir; the building at the far corner."

Ruefully pondering the respectful "sir" from a man no more than seven years his junior, Gersen walked to the end of the mall, threading a many-voiced, many-costumed multitude of students. He crossed the quadrangle, approached the building at the far corner. At the portal he paused, aware of an emotion strangely like diffidence, or shyness,

69

which had gradually been asserting itself during the entire trip out to the university. He jeered at himself. Was he a schoolboy, that the prospect of an evening with a strange girl should give him tremors? And more remarkable, the emotion seemed to take precedence over the basic goal of his existence! He shrugged, irritated and amused together, then entered the foyer.

At a desk a girl looked up, with an uncertainty Gersen identified as equivalent to his own. She was smaller and more slender than he had thought her to be, but by no means less appealing. "Mr. Gersen?"

Gersen put on what he hoped was a reassuring smile. "It occurs to me that I don't know your name."

She relaxed a trifle. "Pallis Atwrode."

"That takes care of the formalities," said Gersen. "I hope that our arrangement is still working?"

She nodded. "Unless you've changed your mind."

"No."

"I act far bolder than I actually am," said Pallis Atwrode. She gave an embarrassed laugh. "I've simply decided to ignore my upbringing. My mother is a blue-stocking. Perhaps it's time I began to overcompensate."

"You begin to alarm me," said Gersen. "I'm not very bold either, and if I have to cope with overcompensation—"

"Not really formidable overcompensation. I won't become intoxicated, or pick a fight, or—" she stopped.

"Or?"

"Oh—just 'or.' "

Gersen looked at his watch. "I'd better see Mr. Warweave."

"His offices are down that corridor. And Mr. Gersen—"

Gersen looked down into the upturned face. "Yes?"

"Today I told you something which it seems I shouldn't have. About the code. It's supposed to be secret. Would you please not mention it to Mr. Warweave? I'd get in trouble."

"I'll say nothing about it."

"Thank you."

He turned, went off down the corridor she had indicated. The floor was resilient black and gray tesserae; the walls and ceiling were plastered white, devoid of decoration or relief except for the various doors and identificators— these in various muted tones of maroon, mauve, dark green, indigo.

Three doors along the corridor Gersen came upon a free-floating identificator of luminous blue letters, which read: GYLE WARWEAVE, and below: PROVOST.

He paused, struck by the incongruity of Malagate the Woe in such surroundings. Was there a break in his chain of reasoning? The monitor was coded, registered to the university. Hildemar Dasce, Malagate's lieutenant, had sought possession of the filament, which was useless without the decoder. Gyle Warweave, Detteras and Kelle were the three men who had access to the decoder, one of the three must be Malagate. So then: which, Warweave, Detteras or Kelle? Conjecture without facts was useless; he must deal with events as they occurred. He stepped forward; the door slipped aside, quick as a camera shutter; the identificator broke into individual letters which scattered like frightened fish, to regroup after he had passed.

In the outer office a tall thin middle-aged woman with keen unsympathetic gray eyes stood listening to an obviously unhappy young man, shaking her head slowly, continually, as he spoke.

"I'm sorry," she said finally, in a clear brittle voice, "these arrangements are all made on a formal basis of student achievement. I can't allow you to bother the provost with your complaints."

"What is he there for, then?" shouted the young man. "He had open office hours; why can't he listen to my side of the story?"

The woman shook her head. "I'm sorry." She turned away. "Are you Mr. Gersen?" she asked.

Gersen came forward.

"Mr. Warweave is expecting you; please go through that door."

Gersen went as directed. Gyle Warweave, sitting at a desk, rose to his feet as Gersen entered: a tall handsome man, strong and fit looking, of an age not immediately obvious —perhaps ten or fifteen years older than Gersen. His hair was a cushion of black curls shaped close to his skull, his skin dye a conservative pale umber. His face was emphatically marked; the eyes narrow, deep-set, black and brooding, the nose and chin harsh. He saluted Gersen with a measured courtesy. "Mr. Gersen, sit down, if you will. I'm glad to make your acquaintance."

Thank you." Gersen looked about him. The room was larger than the usual office, the desk occupying an unconventional position by the left of the door, with the greater part of room beyond. Tall windows at the right overlooked the quadrangle; the opposite wall was papered with hundreds of maps: Mercator projections of many worlds. The center of the room was empty, giving it the semblance of a conference chamber from which the table had been removed. At the far end, on a pedestal of polished wood, stood a construction of stone and metal spires, the provenance of which Gersen was ignorant. He seated himself, returned his attention to the man behind the desk.

Gyle Warweave hardly conformed to Gersen's picture of the typical university administrator. This of course would well be true, thought Gersen, if Warweave were Malagate. Contradicting the evidence of his conservative skin dye, Warweave wore a rich bright-blue suit with a white sash, white leather greaves, pale blue sandals: garments which might be affected by a young buck of the Sailmaker Beach district, north of Avente. . . . Gersen groped at an elusive familiarity, a tantalizing wisp of recollection, which fled completely from view.

Warweave inspected Gersen with a similar frank curiosity, in which there was a trace of condescension. Gersen definitely was no dandy. He wore the neutral garments of a person either uninterested in current modes or unaware of them. His skin was undyed (walking along the streets of Avente, Gersen had felt almost undressed); his thick dark hair was cropped into an undistinguished ruff.

Warweave waited with attentive politeness. Gersen said, "I'm here, Mr. Warweave, in connection with a rather complex matter. My motives are beside the point, so I'll ask you to listen without troubling about them."

Warweave nodded. "Rather difficult, but I'll try."

"First of all, are you acquainted with Mr. Lugo Teehalt?"

"No, I am not." The answer was immediate and decisive.

"May I ask who has the responsibility for the university's space exploration program?"

Warweave considered. "Do you refer to major expeditions, shotgun surveys, or what in particular?"

"Whatever program makes use of locaters in leased boats."

"Hm," said Warweave. He turned a quizzical look toward Gersen. "By any chance, are you a locater in search of a post? If so—"

Gersen smiled politely. "No, I'm not after a job."

Warweave smiled in his turn, a quick humorless grimace. "No, of course not. I'm inept in my judgments. For instance, your voice tells me very little. You're not a native

72

of the Concourse. If you were of a different physiognomy I'd place you from Mizar's Third."

"During most of my youth I lived on Earth."

"Indeed?" Warweave raised his eyebrows in manufactured astonishment. "Out here, you know, we think of Earthmen in terms of stereotypes: cultists, mystics, hypercivilized epicenes, sinister old men in Institute black, decadent aristocrats. . . ."

"I claim no particular niche," said Gersen. "Incidentally, you puzzle me no less than I puzzle you."

Warweave put on an expression of rueful whimsey. "Very well, Mr. Gersen. You were asking about our policy in connection with locaters. First of all, we cooperate with a number of other institutions in the Master Space Exploration Program. Secondly, there is a small fund which may be drawn upon to expedite some special project."

"That is Beneficial Grant 291?"

Warweave inclined his head in curt assent.

"Very odd," said Gersen.

"Odd? How so?"

"Lugo Teehalt was a locater. The monitor in his boat was chartered to Sea Province University, under Grant 291."

Warweave pursed his lips. "It's quite possible that Mr. Teehalt might be working for one of the department heads on some special project."

"The monitor was coded. That should narrow the possibilities."

Warweave pierced Gersen with a hard glance of black eyes. "If I knew what you wanted to learn, I could answer more to the point."

There was nothing to lose by telling at least part of the truth, thought Gersen. If Gyle Warweave were Malagate, he would know what had happened. If he were not, no harm could be done. "The name Attel Malagate is familiar to you?"

"Malagate the Woe? One of the so-called Demon Princes."

"Lugo Teehalt located a world of apparently idyllic conditions—a world literally beyond value, more Earthlike than Earth. Malagate learned of the discovery, how I don't know. In any event, at least four of Malagate's men hunted Teehalt to Smade's Tavern.

"Teehalt arrived just after I did. He landed in a hidden valley and walked to the tavern. During the evening Malagate's men arrived. Teehalt tried to escape, but they caught him in the dark, killed him. Then they took off

73

in my ship, apparently assuming that it was Teehalt's. Both were the same, old Model 9B." Gersen laughed. "When they checked my monitor they had a sorry surprise.

"The next day I left in Teehalt's boat. Naturally I took possession of his monitor. I plan to sell the filament for as much as the market will bear."

Warweave nodded briskly, moved a sheet of paper on his desk an inch to the right. Gersen watched him, studying the immaculate hands, the glossy fingernails. Looking up, he caught the stare of Warweave's gaze, less affable than his tone of voice. "And from whom do you propose to collect?"

Gersen shrugged. "I'll give Teehalt's sponsor the first opportunity. As I mentioned, the filament is coded, and is valueless without the decoding strip."

Warweave leaned back in his chair. "Off-hand I don't know who might have contracted with this man Teehalt. Whoever it is naturally would not buy a pig in a poke."

"Naturally not." Gersen placed a photograph on the desk. Warweave glanced at it, dropped it into a projection slot. A screen on the far wall burst into color. Teehalt had taken the picture from a rise of ground to one side of a valley. On either hand hills rolled back, over, away and beyond—the rounded tips could be seen receding into the distance. Groves of tall dark trees stood to the side of the valley; a river wandered through the meadows, the banks lined with rushes. At the far side of the meadow, almost in the shade of the forest, stood what appeared to be a bank of flowering shrubs. The sun could not be seen, but the sunlight was golden-white, warm, languid, and the time was evidently noon.

Warweave studied the picture at length, then made a gruff noncommittal sound. Gersen provided another photograph; the screen shifted to display the view down the valley: the river meandering and twisting, finally disappearing into the far distance. Trees standing tall at either side formed a sort of aisle, diminishing until all faded into haze.

Warweave heaved a sigh. "Beyond question a beautiful world. A hospitable world. What of atmosphere and biogens?"

"Completely compatible, according to Teehalt."

"If it is as you say—undiscovered, uninhabited—an independent locater could name his own price. Still, not being born yesterday, I wonder, could not this photograph have been made elsewhere? Even on Earth, where the vegetation is similar to this?"

For answer, Gersen brought forth a third photograph.

74

Warweave dropped it into the slot. The screen depicted, as if from a distance of twenty feet, one of the objects which in the first photograph had appeared as a flowering shrub. It was revealed as a perambulatory being, semihumanoid, graceful. Slender gray legs supported a gray, silver, blue, green torso; purple-green eyes looked forth from a perfect ovoid head, which was otherwise featureless. From the shoulders, armlike members reached three feet into the air, branching and webbing, to support the peacock's tail fan of fronds.

"The creature, whatever it is—"

"Teehalt called it a dryad."

"—certainly it is unique. I'v never seen its like before. If the picture is not faked—and I do not believe that it is —then the planet is what you claim it to be."

"I claim nothing. Teehalt made the claims. It is a world —so he told me—so beautiful that he could neither bear to stay nor bear to leave."

"And you have Teehalt's filament in your possession."

"Yes. I want to sell it. The market is presumably limited to those persons who have access to the decoding strip. Of these, the man who sponsored Lugo Teehalt's operation should have the first option."

Warweave gave Gersen a long steady inspection. "A quixotic attitude, which puzzles me. You do not seem a quixotic man."

"Why not judge from deeds rather than impressions?"

Warweave merely raised his eyebrows in something like disdain. Then he said, "Conceivably I could make you an offer for the filament: say two thousand SVU now, another ten thousand after inspection of the world. Possibly a trifle more."

"Naturally I will take the best price I can get," said Gersen. "But I would like to interview Mr. Kelle and Mr. Detteras first. One of them must be Teehalt's sponsor. If neither is interested in the filament, then—"

Warweave interrupted sharply. "Why do you specify these two men?"

"Other than yourself, they are the only persons who have access to the decoding strips."

"May I ask how you are aware of this?"

Remembering Pallis Atwrode's request, Gersen felt a pang of guilt. "I asked a young man in the quadrangle. Apparently it's common knowledge."

"Altogether too much loose talk," said Warweave, his mouth in a hard angry line.

Gersen wanted to inquire how Warweave had spent the previous month, but the occasion was clearly inopportune. It could not be a wise question, if posed directly: if Warweave were Malagate, his suspicion would instantly be reinforced.

Warweave now tapped fingers on his desk, rose to his feet. "If you will give me half an hour I will ask Mr. Detteras and Mr. Kelle to step into my office, and you can make your inquiry. Will that be satisfactory?"

"No."

"No?" barked Warweave. "Why not?"

Gersen also rose to his feet. "Since the matter does not concern you, I would prefer to interview Mr. Kelle and Mr. Detteras alone, on my own terms."

"This is at your option," said Warweave coldly. He considered a moment. "What you are after, I can't guess. I put little faith in your candor. But I will make a bargain with you."

Gersen waited.

"Kelle and Detteras are busy men," said Warweave. "They are not as accessible as I am. I will arrange that you see them at once—today, if you like. Possibly one or the other will admit to an arrangement with Lugo Teehalt. In any case, after your interview with Kelle and Detteras, you will report to me what offers, if any, they have made, and so give me the opportunity of meeting or exceeding the offer."

"In other words," said Gersen, "you'd keep this world for your private use?"

"Why not? The filament is no longer the property of the university. You have taken possession of it. And, if the truth be known, my money has gone to endow Grant 291."

"That's reasonable enough."

"You agree to my bargain, then?"

"Yes. So long as you understand that the first refusal goes to Teehalt's sponsor."

Warweave's eyelids drooped; he inspected Gersen with a rather cynical twist of the lips. "I wonder why you insist on this."

"Perhaps I am a quixotic man after all, Mr. Warweave."

Warweave swung about, spoke into the desk screen, listened, turned back to Gersen. "Very well. Mr. Kelle will see you first, then Mr. Detteras. After that you will report back to me."

"I agree."

"Good. You will find Kelle's office at the opposite end of the building."

Gersen went out into the corridor past Warweave's glint-eyed secretary, returned to the foyer. Pallis Atwrode looked up with an eager expectancy Gersen found very appealing. "Did you learn what you wanted to?"

"No. He's sending me to see Kelle and Detteras."

"Today?"

"Right now."

She looked at him with new interest. "You'd be surprised at the people both Mr. Kelle and Mr. Detteras have refused to see today."

Gersen grinned. "I don't know how long I'll be.... If you're off duty at four—"

"I'll wait," said Pallis Atwrode, and then she laughed. "I mean, you won't be *very* much longer than four, and I'd have to walk home, and explain where I live—it's just easier waiting."

"I'll be as fast as I can," said Gersen.

Chapter 7

Deeming the unsubstantiated dogma of a localized religious cult to be an undignified and unsuitable base on which to erect the chronology of galactic man, the members of this convention hereby declare that time shall now be reckoned from the year 2000 A.D. (Old System), which becomes the year O. The revolution of Earth about Sol remains the standard annual unit.

...Declaration at the Oikumenical Convention for the Standardization of Units and Meters.

"Everything of which we are conscious...has for us a deeper meaning still, a final meaning. And the one and only means of rendering this incomprehensible comprehensible must be a kind of metaphysics which regards *everything whatsoever* as having significance as a symbol."

...Oswald Spengler.

"Who are our basic enemies? This is a secret, unknown even to those basic enemies."

...Xaviar Skolcamp, Over-Centennial Fellow of the Institute, indulgently, in response to a journalist's too-searching question.

* * * * * * *

Kagge Kelle was a small, compact man with a large, solid, well-arranged head. His skin was only faintly dyed, to a waxy bisque pallor; he wore a severe costume of dark brown and purple. His eyes were clear and remote, his nose short and blunt, his mouth prim, held firmly as if in compensation for its overfullness.

Kelle seemed to make a virtue of inscrutability. He greeted Gersen with austere courtesy, listened to his story without comment, saw the photographs without perceptible show of interest. Choosing his words with care, he said, "I am sorry that I cannot help you. I did not sponsor Mr. Teehalt's expedition. I know nothing about this man."

"In that case, will you allow me the use of the decoding strip?"

Kelle sat motionless for a moment. Then he said in an even voice, "unfortunately, this is contrary to the rules of the department. I would encounter not a little criticism. Still. . . . " He picked up the photographs, examined them once more. "This is beyond question a world of interesting characteristics. What is its name?"

"I don't have that information, Mr. Kelle."

"I cannot conceive why you seek Teehalt's sponsor. Are you a representative of the IPCC?"

"I am a private individual, though naturally I can't demonstrate this."

Kelle was skeptical. "Everyone works to his own interests. If I understood what you were trying to achieve, I could possibly act with more flexibility."

"That is more or less what Mr. Warweave told me," said Gersen.

Kelle turned on him a sharp look. "Neither Warweave nor myself are what might be called innocent men." He thought for a moment, then said grudgingly, "On behalf of the department, I can go so far as to make you an offer for the filament—though, as you tell the story, it actually is the property of the department to begin with."

Gersen nodded in full agreement. "That is exactly the point I am trying to establish. Does the filament actually belong to the university, or can I feel free to do as I like with it? If I could find Lugo Teehalt's sponsor—or determine whether the sponsor actually exists—then any number of new possibilities would appear."

Kelle was not to be moved by Gersen's ingenuousness. "It is an extraordinary situation . . . As I say, I might be able to make you an attractive offer for the filament—even as a private party, if that would expedite matters. Although I would naturally insist on a prior inspection of the planet."

"You know my qualms in the matter, Mr. Kelle."

Kelle's response was only a small incredulous smile. Once more he studied the photographs. "These—er, dryads, I must say they are creatures of considerable interest. . . . Well, I can help you to this extent. I will consult university records for information regarding Lugo Teehalt. But in exchange, I would like you to assure me an opportunity to consider the purchase of this world, in the event that you do not find the so-called 'sponsor.' "

Gersen could not restrain a mild gibe. "You gave me to understand that you weren't particularly interested."

"Your assumptions are of no consequence," said Kelle evenly. "This should not injure your sensibilities, for you clearly are not concerned as to my opinion of you. You approach me as if I were mentally deficient, with a tale which would not impress a child."

Gersen shrugged. "The 'tale,' as it stands, is substantially accurate. Naturally I haven't told you everything I know."

Kelle smiled again, rather more generously. "Well, let's see what the records have to tell us." He spoke into the microphone. "Confidential Information. Authority of Kagge Kelle."

The nonhuman voice of the information bank responded. "Confidential Information, ready."

"The file on Lugo Teehalt." He spelled out the name.

There was a series of subdued mutterings, a quiet eerie whistling. The voice spoke once more, reading off the information it had gathered. "Lugo Teehalt: his file. Contents: Application for admission, verification and appended comment. April 3, 1480."

"Pass," said Kelle.

"Application for admission to advanced regimen, verification and appended comment. July 2, 1485."

"Pass."

"Thesis for degree in College of Symbology: title: 'The Meaningful Elements in the Eye Motion of the Tunkers of Mizar Six.' December 20, 1489."

"Pass."

"Application for post as associate instructor, verification and comment. March 15, 1490."

"Discharge of Lugo Teehalt, associate instructor, for conduct prejudicial to morale of student corpus. October 19, 1492."

"Pass."

"Contract between Lugo Teehalt and Department of Galactic Morphology, January 6, 1521."

Gersen exhaled a small sigh at the relaxation of tension of whose existence he had barely been aware. It was definite:

Lugo Teehalt had been employed as locater by someone within the department.

"Quote in resumé," Kelle ordered.

"Lugo Teehalt and Department of Galactic Morphology agree and covenant to the following: Department will furnish Teehalt a suitable space vessel, provisioned, equipped, found in typical and useful manner, in order that Teehalt shall conduct, as agent of department, assiduous exploration of certain areas of galaxy. Department advances Teehalt sum of five thousand SVU and guarantees a bonus of graduated values for degrees of successful exploration. Teehalt agrees to devote best efforts to successful pursuit of exploration, to preserve results of said exploration secure and secret from all persons, groups, and agencies other than those authorized by Department. Signatures: Lugo Teehalt for Lugo Teehalt; Ominah Bazerman for department.

"No further information."

"Mmf," said Kagge Kelle. He spoke to the screen. "Ominah Bazerman."

A click, a voice spoke. "Ominah Bazerman, Chief Clerk."

"Kelle speaking. Two years ago a certain Lugo Teehalt was despatched as a locater. You signed his contract. Do you remember the circumstances?"

There was a moment's silence. "No, Mr. Kelle, I can't say that I do. The contract probably came to me in a set of other papers."

"You don't remember who would have initiated this contract, who sponsored this particular exploration?"

"No, sir. It must have been either yourself, or Mr. Detteras, or perhaps Mr. Warweave. No one else would order out such an exploration."

"I see. Thank you." Kelle turned to Gersen, his eyes mild, almost bovine. "And there you have it. If it wasn't Warweave, it must be Detteras. As a matter of fact Detteras is former Dean of the College of Symbology. Perhaps he and Teehalt were acquaintances. . . ."

* * * * * * * *

Rundle Detteras, Director of Exploration, seemed a man

80

completely at his ease—at peace with himself, his job, the world at large. When Gersen entered his office, Detteras held up his hand in easy salute. He was a large man, surprisingly ugly for this age when a pointed nose or an overloose mouth could be repaired in a matter of hours. He had made no attempt to camouflage his ugliness; indeed, it seemed as if his rather harsh blue-green skin dye, almost the color of verdigris, accentuated the coarseness of his features, the rather gauche brusqueness of his motions. His head was the shape of a gourd; the heavy chin rested on his breast with no perceptible intervention of neck, the hair was a bristle dyed the color of wet moss. From knee to shoulder he seemed of uniform thickness, with a torso like a log. He wore the quasimilitary uniform of a Baron of the Order of Archangels: black boots, loose scarlet breeches, and a splendid blouse striped green, blue and scarlet, with gold epaulettes and filigreed breast plates. Rundle Detteras was of sufficient presence to command both the uniform and his odd physiognomy; a man with the slightest dubiety or self-consciousness would instantly have seemed eccentric.

"Well, well, Mr. Gersen," said Detteras, "is it too early for a taste of arrack?"

"I'm out of bed."

Detteras stared in brief puzzlement, then laughed heartily. "Excellent! This is when I usually hoist the hospitality flag. Tint, tang, or white?"

"White, please."

Detteras poured from the tall slender flask. He raised his glass: "Detteras *au pouvoir!*" and drank with gusto. "First of the day, like a visit home to mother." He poured himself a second tot, settled back, turned upon Gersen a glance of leisurely appraisal. Gersen asked himself, which one: Warweave? Kelle? Detteras? One of these exteriors hid the ferocious soul of Attel Malagate the Woe. Warweave? Kelle? Detteras? Gersen had inclined toward Warweave; now he was once more dubious. Detteras had undeniable force, a rude, harsh-textured energy, almost palpable.

Detteras apparently felt no urgency about coming to grips with Gersen's business, for all the reputed press of his affairs. It was not unlikely that he and Warweave had been in communication, and possibly Kelle likewise. "A never-ending puzzle," said Detteras, rather pompously. "The modes of why and how men differ."

If Detteras were in no hurry, thought Gersen, neither was

81

he. "No doubt you're right," he said, "although I don't understand the immediate relevance."

Detteras laughed: a heavy booming sound. "Quite as it should be; I would be surprised if you professed otherwise." He held up his hand to forestall Gersen's response. "Presumption on my part? No. Hear me out. You are a somber man, a pragmatic man. You carry a heavy load of secrets and dark resolves."

Gersen sipped suspiciously at the arrack. The verbal pyrotechnics might be intended as a distraction, a device to diminish his wariness. He concentrated on the arrack, senses keen for the faintest off flavor. Detteras had poured both drinks from the same flask; he had offered Gersen a choice of three distillations; he had taken up glasses without seeming calculation. There existed, nonetheless, enormous scope for ruse, which no normal vigilance could prevent. . . . The drink was innocent, so Gersen's tongue and nasal passages, trained on Sarkovy, assured him. He focused his attention upon Detteras and the previous remark.

"Your opinions regarding me are exaggerated."

Detteras grinned, a great gap-lipped grimace. "But nevertheless essentially accurate?"

"Possibly."

Detteras nodded complacently, as if Gersen had given him the most emphatic of corroborations. "It is a skill, or habit of observation, born of long years of study. I formerly specialized in Symbology, until I decided that I'd cropped the pasture as short as my teeth were long, and as far as my tether would reach. So here I am in Galactic Morphology. A less complicated field, descriptive rather than analytic, objective rather than humanistic. Still, I occasionally find application for my previous field. Now is a case in point. You come into my office, an utter stranger. I assess your overt symbolic presentation: skin color; shape, condition, color of your hair; features, clothes, your general style. You will say, this is common practice. I reply, true. Everyone eats, but a skilled taster is rare. I read these symbols with minute exactitude, and they provide me with information about your personality. I, on the other hand, deny similar knowledge to you. How? I bedizen myself with random and contradictory symbols, I am in constant camouflage, behind which the real Rundle Detteras watches, as calm and cool as an impresario at the hundredth performance of a glittering carnival extravaganza."

Gersen smiled. "My nature might be as flamboyant as your

82

symbols, and I might dissemble it for reasons similar to your own—whatever they are. A second point: your presentation, if it can be believed, illuminated you almost as clearly as the set of your natural symbols. Third—why bother in the first place?"

Detteras seemed much amused. "Aha! You show me for the fraud and charlatan I am! Still, I cannot avoid the conviction that your symbols tell me more about you than mine do about me."

Gersen leaned back in his seat. "To little practical effect."

"Not so fast," exclaimed Detteras. "You occupy yourself exclusively with positivity! Consider negativity for a moment. Some people fret regarding the cryptic mannerisms of their colleagues. You protest that the symbols tell you nothing of importance; you dismiss them. These others worry because they cannot integrate a proliferation of information." Gersen started to demur; Detteras held up his hand. "Consider the Tunkers of Mizar Six. You are acquainted with them? A religious sect."

"I heard them mentioned a few minutes ago."

"As I say," Detteras continued, "they are a religious group: ascetic, austere, devout to an astonishing extreme. The men and women dress identically, shave their heads, use a language of eight hundred and twelve words, eat identical meals at identical hours—all this to protect themselves from the perplexity of wondering about each other's motivations. True. This is the basic purpose of the Tunker mode. And not too far from Mizar is Sirene, where for a similar reason men wear highly conventionalized masks, from birth to death. Their faces are their dearest secrets." He proffered the arrack flask. Gersen held out his glass.

Detteras continued. "The practice here on Alphanor is more complicated. We gird ourselves for offense and defense, or sheer playfulness, with a thousand ambiguous symbols. The business of living is enormously complicated; artificial tensions are established; uncertainty and suspicion become normality."

"And in the process," suggested Gersen, "sensitivities are developed unknown to either the Tunkers or the Sirenese."

Detteras held up his hand. "Again, not so fast. I know a great deal about both these peoples; insensitivity is a word which cannot be applied to either. The Sirenese will detect the most remote nuance of uneasiness when a man masks himself above his status. And the Tunkers—I know less of them, but I believe that their personal differentiations are as

83

refined and varied as our own, if not more so. I quote an analogous esthetic doctrine: the tighter the discipline of an art form, the more subjective the criteria of taste. In another category, becoming ever more didactic, consider the Star Kings—nonmen driven by their psyches to literally superhuman excellences. They must enter the field cold, as it were, without even the human racial unconscious as a matrix for their symbolic education. Returning to Alphanor, it must be remembered that the folk thrust an enormous amount of perfectly valid information at each other, as well as ambiguities."

"Confusing," said Gersen dryly, "if one allows himself to be distracted."

Detteras laughed quietly, evidently well pleased with himself. "You've led a different life than I have, Mr. Gersen. On Alphanor the issues aren't life and death; everyone is fairly sophisticated. It's easier than not to accept people at their own valuation. Indeed, it's often impractical not to do so." He looked sidelong at Gersen. "Why do you smile?"

"It dawns upon me that the dossier on Kirth Gersen, requested from the IPCC, is slow in arriving. In the meantime, you find it impractical to accept me at my own valuation. Or even your own."

Detteras laughed in his turn. "You do both me and the IPCC an injustice. The dossier came promptly, several minutes before your arrival." He pointed to a photostat sheet on his desk. "I ordered the dossier, incidentally, in my role as a responsible officer of the Institution. I think I can make a case for my caution."

"What did you learn?" asked Gersen. "I haven't seen the dossier recently."

"It's marvelously blank." He picked up the paper. "You were born in 1490: where? Not on one of the major worlds. At the age of ten you registered into Galileo Spaceport on Earth, in the company of your grandfather, whose antecedents perhaps we should likewise check. You attended the usual schools, were accepted by the Institute as a catechumen, reached the eleventh phase at the age of twenty-four (quite respectable progress), when you withdrew. From now on there is no record, suggesting that either you remained permanently on Earth, or departed illegally, without registration. Since you now sit before me, the latter seems to have been the case. Remarkable," said Detteras, "that a person could live to your age in a society as complex as the Oikumene with no small impingement upon the official

84

record! Long years of silence while you were occupied where? How? To what purpose, and to what effect?" He glanced questioningly at Gersen.

"If it's not there," said Gersen, "I don't want it there."

"Naturally. There is very little more." He tossed down the dossier. "Now you are anxious to make your inquiries. I will anticipate you. I knew Lugo Teehalt, far back indeed, in my undergraduate days. He involved himself in some sort of unsavory mess and dropped from sight. A year or so ago he came to me, asking for a locater's contract."

Gersen stared at him, fascinated. So here was Malagate! "And you sent him out?"

"I chose not to do so. I did not want him dependent upon me for the rest of his life. I was willing to help him, but not on a personal basis. I told him to apply either to the Honorary Provost, Gyle Warweave, or the Chairman of the Research Planning Committee, Kagge Kelle; to mention my name, that very likely they could assist him. This was the last I heard of him."

Gersen took a deep breath. Detteras spoke with the assurance of truth. But which of them had not? Detteras at least had confirmed that one of the three—either himself, Warweave or Kelle—was lying.

Which?

Today he had seen Attel Malagate, looked into his eyes, listened to his voice. . . . He was suddenly uneasy. Why was Deterras so relaxed? Presumably a busy man, how could he spare so much time? Gersen abruptly sat up in his chair. "I will get to the point of my call upon you." He told the story he had already related to Warweave and Kelle, while Detteras listened with a faint smile playing over his coarse mouth. Gersen displayed the photographs and Detteras looked at them negligently.

"A beautiful world," said Detteras. "If I were wealthy I would ask you to sell it to me to be my personal estate. I am not wealthy. On the contrary. In any event, you seem not so much anxious to sell your rights to this world as you do to locate poor old Teehalt's sponsor."

Gersen was somewhat taken aback. "I'll sell to the sponsor for a reasonable price."

Detteras smiled skeptically. "Sorry. I can't admit to a falsehood. Warweave or Kelle is your man."

"They deny it."

"Strange. So then?"

"The filament is useless to me in its present condition. Will you furnish me the decoding strip?"

"I'm afraid that's out of the question."

"I thought as much. So I must sell to one or the other of you, or to the university. Or destroy the filament."

"Hm." Detteras judiciously nodded his head. "This demands careful thought. If your demands were not excessive, I'd be interested. . . . Or perhaps the three of us, in concert, could come to some agreement with you. Hm. . . . Let me speak to Warweave and Kelle. And then, if you can, come back tomorrow, say at ten. I might have a definite proposition to put before you."

Gersen rose to his feet. "Very well. Tomorrow at ten."

Chapter 8

"Yes, we are a reactionary, secretive, pessimistic organization. We have agents everywhere. We know a thousand tricks to discourage research, sabotage experiments, distort data. Even in the Institute's own laboratories we proceed with deliberation and discretion.

"But now let me answer some of the questions and accusations we often hear. Do the members of the Institute enjoy wealth, privilege, power, freedom from the law? Honesty compels the answer: Yes, in varying degree, depending upon phase, achievement.

"Then the Institute is an in-bred, restricted, centripetal group? By no means. We consider ourselves an intellectual elite, certainly. Why should we not? Membership is open to anyone, although few of our catechumens achieve even so far as the fifth phase.

"Our policy? Simple enough. Space drive has given a terrible weapon to any megalomaniacs who happen to occur in our midst. There is other knowledge which, if equally free, could ensure them tyrannical power. We therefore control the dissemination of knowledge.

"We are scathed as 'self-anointed divinities'; we are accused of pedantry, conspiracy, condescension, smugness, arrogance, obstinate self-righteousness: these are the mildest of the objurgations we hear. We are accused of intolerable paternalism, and in the same breath reproached for disengagement from or-

86

dinary human affairs. Why do we not use our lore to lighten toil, alleviate pain, prolong life? Why do we stand aloof? Why do we not transform the human estate into a utopia: a task well within our power?

"The answer is simple—perhaps deceptively so. We feel these are false boons; that peace and satiety are akin to death. For all its rawness and cruel excess, we envy archaic humanity its ardent experience. We hold that gain after toil, triumph after adversity, achievement to a goal long sought, is a greater beneficence than prebendary nutrient from the teat of an indulgent government."

... From the television address by Madian Carbuke, Centennial (Hundredth Phase Fellow) of the Institute, December 2, 1502.

Conversation between two Centennials of the Institute, in connection with a third not present:

—"I would gladly come to your house for a chat, if I did not suspect that Ramus were likewise invited."

—"But what is so wrong with Ramus? He often amuses me."

—"He is a fungus, a flatulence, a pompous old toad, and he irritates me vastly."

Question occasionally put to Fellows of the Institute: Are Star Kings included among the fellowship?

The customary answer: We certainly hope not.

Motto of the Institute: *A little knowledge is a dangerous thing; a great deal of knowledge is disaster*, which detractors of the Institute scornfully paraphrase to: *Somebody else's ignorance is bliss.*

* * * * * * *

Pallis Atwrode lived with two other girls in a seaside apartment tower to the south of Remo. Gersen waited in the lobby while she ran up to change clothes and retint her skin.

He went out on the deck overlooking the ocean, leaned against the rail. Great blazing Rigel hung low over the ocean, laying a molten road from shore to horizon. Near at hand in the harbor, enclosed by twin piers, a hundred boats were moored: power yachts, sailing catamarans, glass-hulled submarines, a shoal of jet-powered aquaplanes, to be ridden at maniacal speed over, through, and across the waves.

87

Gersen's mood was complex, and puzzled even himself. There was the heart-bumping anticipation of an evening with a pretty girl, a sensation he had not known for years. There was the melancholy normally induced by sunset—and now the sunset was beautiful indeed; the sky glowed mauve and green-blue around a green bank of persimmon-orange clouds stranded with magenta. It was not the beauty which brought on melancholy, mused Gersen, but rather the quiet halcyon light and its fading. . . . And there was another melancholy —different yet somehow similar—which came to Gersen as he watched the debonair folk about him. They were all graceful and easy, untouched by the toil and pain and terror that existed on remote worlds. Gersen envied them their detachment, their social skills. Still, would he change places with any of them? Hardly.

Pallis Atwrode came to join him by the rail. She had tinted herself a beautiful soft olive-green, with a subtle patina of gold; she now wore her hair in a loose dark curly cap. She laughed at Gersen's obvious approval.

"I feel like a wharf rat," said Gersen. "I should have changed into new clothes."

"Please don't worry," she said. "It's completely unimportant. Now. What shall we do?"

"You'll have to make suggestions."

"Very well. Let's go into Avente and sit on the esplanade. I never tire of watching people walk past. Then we can decide what's next."

Gersen acceded; they walked to the slide car and drove north, Pallis chattering with ingenuous candor about herself, her job, her opinions, plans and hopes. She was, so Gersen learned, a native of Singhal Island, on the planet Ys. Her parents were prosperous, owning the only cold-storage warehouse of the Lantango Peninsula. When they retired to the Palmetto Islands, her oldest brother took control of the warehouse and likewise the family home. The brother next older had wished to marry her, this form of union being countenanced on Ys, which had been settled originally by a group of Reformed Rationalists. The brother was stout, red-faced, arrogant, without a trade other than driving the warehouse van, and the prospect held no charm for Pallis. . . .

At this point Pallis hesitated and her candor seemed to slip gears, for she changed the subject. Gersen guessed at the dramatic confrontations, fierce reproaches and countering accusations which had taken place. Pallis had now lived in Avente for two years and, though sometimes homesick for the sights and sounds of Ys, she felt herself happy and lucky. Gersen, who had never known anyone so artless, was charmed by her talk.

They parked the slider, walked out along the esplanade, selected a table in front of one of the numerous cafés, and sat watching the crowds stroll by. Beyond spread the dark ocean, with the sky now plum and indigo-gray, with only the faintest tinge of lemon to mark the passage of Rigel.

The night was warm; folk from all the worlds of the Oikumene sauntered past. The waiter brought goblets of punch. Gersen sipped and his tensions began to relax. Neither spoke for a period; then Pallis suddenly turned to face him. "You're so silent, so guarded; is it because you're in from Beyond?"

Gersen had no ready reply. Finally he gave a rueful laugh. "I hoped you'd think me easy and suave, like everyone else. . . ."

"Oh come now," said Pallis teasingly. "Nobody's like everyone else."

"I'm not altogether sure," said Gersen. "I suppose it's a matter of relativity: how near you are. Even bacteria have individuality, if they're examined closely enough."

"So now I'm a bacterium," said Pallis.

"Well, I'm another, and I'm probably boring you."

"No, no! Of course not! I'm enjoying myself."

"So am I. Too much. It's—enervating."

Pallis scented a compliment. "How do you mean?"

"I can't allow myself the luxury of emotional commitments—even if I should like to."

"You're much, much, much too sober for a young man."

"I'm not young any more."

She made a gay gesture. "But you admit you're sober!"

"I suppose so. But be careful, don't push me too far."

"A woman likes to think herself a temptress."

Again Gersen had no response. He studied Pallis across the table; for the moment she seemed content to watch the passersby. What a gay, warm-hearted creature, he thought, without a trace of malice or acerbity.

Pallis turned her attention back to him. "You're really such a quiet man," she told him. "Everyone else I know refuses to stop talking, and I listen to continual floods of nonsense. I'm sure you know hundreds of interesting things, and you refuse to tell me any of them."

Gersen grinned. "They're probably less interesting than you think."

"Still, I'd like to make sure. So tell me about the Beyond. Is life really so dangerous?"

"Sometimes yes, sometimes no. It depends on whom you meet, and why."

"But—perhaps you'd rather I didn't ask—what do you do? You're not a pirate or a slaver?"

"Do I look like a pirate? Or a slaver?"

"You know that I don't know what a pirate or a slaver look like! But I'm curious. Are you a—well, criminal? Not that it's necessarily a disgrace," she added hastily. "Affairs which are perfectly acceptable on one planet are absolutely taboo on another. For instance, I told one of my friends that all my life I'd planned to marry my oldest brother—and her hair uncurled!"

"I'm sorry to disappoint you," said Gersen, "but I'm not a criminal. . . . I don't fit into any category." He considered. There could be no indiscretion in telling her what he had told Warweave, Kelle and Detteras. "I've come to Avente for a particular purpose, naturally—"

"Let's have dinner," said Pallis, "and you can tell me while we eat."

"Where shall we go?"

"There's an exciting new restaurant, only just opened. Everyone's talking about it and I've never been there." She jumped to her feet, took his hand with an easy intimacy, pulled him upright. He caught him under the arms, bent forward, but his daring waned; he laughed and released her. She said archly, "You're more impulsive than you look."

Gersen grinned, half shamefacedly. "Well, where is the exciting new restaurant?"

"Not far. We can walk. It's rather expensive, but I plan to pay half the account."

"That's not necessary," said Gersen. "Money is no particular problem to a pirate. If I run short, I'll rob someone. You, perhaps. . . ."

"It's hardly worth the trouble. Come along, then." She took his hand, and they walked north along the esplanade like any of the thousand other couples abroad this fine Alphanor evening.

She led him to a kiosk circled by large luminous green letters reading NAUTILUS. An escalator dropped them two hundred feet into a tall octagonal lobby paneled with rattan screens. A major domo escorted them along a glass-vaulted tunnel, out upon the floor of the sea. Dining rooms of various sizes opened off the passage, into one of which

90

they were conducted, and seated at a table close beside the sloping glass dome. The sea lay beyond, with beacons illuminating the sand, rocks, seaweed, coral, the passing submarine creatures.

"Now," said Pallis, leaning forward, "tell me about the Beyond. And don't worry about alarming me, because I love an occasional shudder. Or better, tell me about yourself."

"Smade's Tavern on Smade's Planet is a good place to start," said Gersen. "You've been there?"

"Of course not. But I've heard it mentioned."

"It's a small, barely habitable planet out in the middle of nowhere: all mountains, wind, thunderstorms, an ocean black as ink. The tavern is the only building on the planet. Sometimes it's crowded, sometimes there'll be no one but Smade and his family for weeks on end. When I arrived the only other guest was a Star King."

"A Star King? I thought they were always disguised as men."

"It's not a matter of disguise," said Gersen. "They *are* men. Almost."

"I never have understood about the Star Kings. Just what are they?"

Gersen shrugged. "You'll get a different answer every time you ask. The general speculation goes like this. A million years ago, more or less, the planet Lambda Grus III, or 'Ghnarumen'—you have to cough through your nose to get it even approximately right—was inhabited by a rather frightening assortment of creatures. Among them was a small amphibious biped without any particular tools for survival except awareness and an ability to hide in the mud. He probably looked a little like a lizard, or a hairless seal. . . . The species faced extinction half a dozen times, but a few always managed to hang on, and somehow scavenge an existence among creatures who were more savage, more cunning, more agile, better swimmers, better climbers, even better scavengers than themselves. The proto-Star Kings had only physical advantages: self-consciousness, competitiveness, a desire to stay alive by any means whatever."

"They sound rather like the proto-humans on ancient Earth," said Pallis.

"No one knows for sure: at least no men. What the Star Kings know they're not telling. . . . These bipeds differed from proto-man in several respects: first, they are biologically much more flexible, able to transmit acquired characteristics. Sec-

91

ond, they are not bisexual. There is cross-fertilization by means of spores emitted on the breath, but each individual is male and female at once, and the young develop as pods in the armpits. Perhaps from this lack of sexual differentiation the Star Kings have no natural physical vanity. Their basic drive is the urge to outdo, to outfunction, to outsurvive. The biological flexibility coupled to a rudimentary intelligence provided the means to implement their ambitions; they consciously began to breed themselves into a creature which could outperform their less resourceful competitors.

"This is all speculation, of course, and what follows is speculation on an even more tenuous basis. But just let's assume that some race able to traverse space visited Earth. It might have been the people which left ruins on the Fomalhaut planets, or the Hexadelts, or whoever carved Monument Cliff on Xi Puppis X.

"We assume that such a space-traveling people came by Earth a hundred thousand years ago. Assume that they captured a tribe of Mousterian Neanderthals, and for some reason conveyed them to Ghnarumen, world of the proto-Star Kings. Here is a challenging situation for both parties. The men are far more dangerous opponents to the Star Kings than the now-defeated natural enemies. The men are intelligent, patient, crafty, ruthless, aggressive. Under pressure of the environment the men themselves evolve into a different type: more agile, faster of body and mind than their Neanderthal predecessors.

"The proto-Star Kings suffer setbacks, but they have their hereditary patience, as well as important weapons: the competitive urge, the biological flexibility. Men have proved superior to themselves; to compete with men they shape themselves into human semblance.

"The war continues, and the Star Kings admit, very guardedly, that certain of their myths describe these wars.

"Another assumption now becomes necessary. About fifty thousand years ago the space travelers return, and convey the evolved Earthmen back to Earth, and perhaps a few Star Kings: who knows? And so the Cro-Magnons appear in Europe."

"On their own planet the Star Kings are at last more manlike than men, and prevail: the true men are destroyed, the Star Kings are supreme and remain so until five hundred years ago. The men of Earth discover the intersplit. When they chance upon "Ghnarumen' they are astonished to find creatures exactly resembling themselves: the Star Kings."

92

"It sounds far-fetched," said Pallis dubiously.

"Not as far-fetched as convergent evolution. It is a fact that Star Kings exist: a race not antagonistic, but not friendly either. Men are not allowed to visit 'Ghnarumen'—or however the name is pronounced. The Star Kings tell us only as much about themselves as they care to, and they send observers—spies, if you like—everywhere throughout the Oikumene. There are probably a dozen Star Kings in Avente right now."

Pallis grimaced. "How can you tell them from men?"

"Sometimes even a doctor can't, after they finish disguising and faking themselves. There are differences, of course. They have no genital organs; their pubic region is blank. Their protoplasm, blood, hormones have a different composition. Their breath has a distinctive odor. But the spies, or whatever they are, are altered so that even an X-ray shows the same as that of a man."

"How did you know the—the creature at Smade's Tavern was a Star King?"

"Smade told me."

"How did Smade know?"

Gersen shook his head. "I never thought to ask."

He sat silent, preoccupied with a new notion. There had been three guests at Smade's Tavern: himself, Teehalt, and the Star King. If Tristano were to be believed—and why not? —he had arrived in company only with Dasce and Suthiro. If Dasce's statement to Teehalt were to be credited, Attel Malagate must be reckoned Teehalt's murder. Gersen had certainly heard Teehalt's scream while Suthiro, Dasce and Tristano stood within his range of vision.

Unless Smade were Malagate, unless another ship had surreptitiously arrived—which were both unlikely—then Malagate and the Star King must be one. Thinking back, Gersen recalled that the Star King had left the dining hall in ample time to allow a conference outside with Dasce. . . .

Pallis Atwrode lightly touched his cheek. "You were telling me of Smade's Tavern."

"Yes," said Gersen. "So I was." He looked at her speculatively. She must certainly know a great deal about the comings and goings of Warweave, Kelle and Detteras. Pallis, misunderstanding the nature of his gaze, flushed prettily under her pale-green skin toning. Gersen laughed uneasily. "Back to Smade's Tavern." He described the events of the evening.

Pallis listened with interest, almost forgetting to eat. "So now you have Lugo Teehalt's filament and the university has the decoder."

"Correct. And neither one is valuable without the other."

They finished dinner; Gersen, with no credit account on Alphanor, paid the bill in cash. They returned to the surface. "Now what would you like?"

"I don't care," said Pallis. "Let's go back along the esplanade to a table, for a while, anyway."

The night was now dark: the moonless black-velvet night of Alphanor. The façade of every building at the back of the esplanade glowed faintly, blue or green or pink; the pavement gave off a silver effulgence; the balustrade emitted a pleasant, almost unseen amber-beige radiance; everywhere was soft shadowless light, rich with muted ghost color. Up in the dark sky stars floated, big, vague, pale. A waiter brought coffee and liqueur; they settled back to watch the passing crowds.

Pallis said in a reflective voice, "You're not telling me everything."

"Of course not," said Gersen. "In fact. . . ." He paused, grappling with a disturbing new thought. Attel Malagate might mistake the nature of his interest in Pallis—especially if Malagate were a Star King, sexless, unable to understand the male-female relationship. "In fact," said Gersen in a bleak voice, "I really have no right involving you in my troubles."

"I don't feel involved," said Pallis, stretching her arms lazily. "And if I were, what of it? This is Avente on Alphanor, a civilized city on a civilized planet."

Gersen gave a sardonic chuckle. "I told you that others were interested in my planet. Well—these others are pirates and slavers as depraved as your romantic heart could desire. . . . Have you ever heard of Attel Malagate?"

"Malagate the Woe? Yes."

Gersen resisted the temptation of telling her that she took messages and ran errands daily for Malagate. "It's almost certain," he said, "that stick-tights are watching us. Now. This very minute. And the other end of the circuit is possibly Malagate himself."

Pallis moved uneasily, scanned the sky. "Do you mean that Malagate is watching me? That's a creepy feeling."

Gersen looked to right, to left, then stared. Two tables away sat Suthiro, the Sarkoy venefice. Gersen felt a sinking at the pit of his stomach. Meeting Gersen's eye, Suthiro nodded politely, smiled. He rose to his feet, sauntered to the table.

"Good evening, Mr. Gersen."

"Good evening," said Gersen.

"May I join you?"

"I'd prefer not."

Suthiro laughed softly, seated himself, inclined his fox face toward Pallis. "And this young lady—do you plan to introduce me?"

"You already know who she is."

"But she does not know me."

Gersen turned to Pallis. "Here you see Scop Suthiro, Master Venefice of Sarkovy. You expressed an interest in evil men; here you have as completely evil a man as you're likely to meet."

Suthiro laughed in easy glee. "Mr. Gersen judiciously uses the word 'likely.' Certain of my friends surpass me as grandly as I surpass you. I hope indeed that you do not meet them. Hildemar Dasce, for instance, who boasts of his ability to paralyze dogs with a glance."

Pallis' voice was troubled: "I'd just as soon not meet him." She stared at Suthiro in fascination. "You really—admit that you're evil?"

Suthiro laughed once more, a subtle muffled sound. "I am a man; I am a Sarkoy."

Gersen said, "I've just been describing our encounter at Smade's Tavern to Miss Atwrode. Tell me something: Who killed Lugo Teehalt?"

Suthiro seemed surprised. "Who else but Malagate? We three sat within. Does it make any difference? It might as easily have been myself or Beauty or Tristano. . . . Tristano, by the way, is quite ill. He suffered a dreadful accident, but hopes to see you on his recovery."

"He can consider himself lucky," said Gersen.

"He is ashamed," said Suthiro. "He thinks himself skillful. I have told him he is not so skillful as I. Now perhaps he will believe it."

"Speaking of skill," said Gersen, "can you do the paper trick?"

Suthiro cocked his head sidewise. "Yes, of course. Where did you learn of the paper trick?"

"At Kalvaing."

"And what wrought you at Kalvaing?"

"A visit with Coudirou the venefice."

Suthiro pursed his heavy red lips. He wore a yellow skin tone; his brown pelt was glossy and smooth with oil. "Coudirou is as wise as any—but as for the paper trick. . . ." Gersen handed him a napkin. Suthiro suspended it from left thumb and forefinger, stroked it lightly with his right hand. It fell to the table in five ribbons.

"Well done," said Gersen, and to Pallis: "His fingernails are hardened, sharp as razors. Naturally he would waste no poison on the paper, but each of his fingers is like the head of a serpent."

Surhiro made complacent acquiescence.

Gersen turned back to him. "Where is your friend Fancy Dasce?"

"Not too far distant."

"Red face and all?"

Suthiro shook his head sadly at Dasce's poor taste in skin toning. "A very able, a very strange man. Have you ever wondered about his face?"

"When I could bear to look at it."

"You are not my friend, you tricked me beautifully; nevertheless, I will warn you: never cross Fancy Dasce. Twenty years ago he was thwarted in some small escapade. It was a matter of collecting money from an obstinate man. Hildemar by chance found himself at a disadvantage. He was knocked down and strapped hand and foot. So his creditor had the poor taste to cleave poor Hildemar's nose, and cut off his eyelids. . . . Hildemar eventually escaped and now is known as Beauty Dasce, or Fancy Dasce."

"How awful," muttered Pallis.

"Exactly." Suthiro's voice became contemptuous. "A year later Hildemar allowed himself the luxury of capturing this man. He conveyed him to a private place, where he lives to this day. And occasionally Hildemar, remembering the outrage which cost him his features, returns to this private place to remonstrate with the man."

Pallis turned glazed eyes at Gersen. "These people are your friends?"

"No. We are associated only through Lugo Teehalt." Suthiro was looking along the esplanade. Gersen asked idly, "You and Dasce and Tristano work together and train together as a team?"

"Often, though I for one prefer a singular scope."

"And Lugo Teehalt had the misfortune to blunder upon you at Brinktown."

"He died quickly. Godogma takes all men. Is this misfortune?"

"One never likes to hasten Godogma."

"True." Suthiro inspected his strong agile hands. "Agreed."

He looked toward Pallis. "On Sarkovy we have a thousand popular aphorisms to this effect."

"Who is Godogma?"

"The Great God of Destiny, who carries a flower and a flail, and walks on wheels."

Gersen put on an air of studious concentration. "I will ask you a question. You need not answer; in fact perhaps you do not know. But I am puzzled: Why should Malagate, a Star King, so vehemently desire this particular world?"

Suthiro shrugged. "That is a matter with which I have never concerned myself. Apparently the world is valuable. I am paid. I kill only when I must or when it profits me— so you see," he told Pallis parenthetically, "I am not really so evil a man, am I now? Presently I will return to Sarkovy and live out my days roaming the Gorobundur Steppe. Ah, now! There is the life! When I think of those times to come, I wonder why I sit here now, beside this odious wetness." He grimaced toward the sea, and rose to his feet. "It is a presumption to advise you, but why not be sensible? You can never defeat Malagate; therefore relinquish the filament."

Gersen thought for a moment, then said, "I will also presume, in the same spirit which prompts you. My advice is this: Kill Hildemar Dasce the next moment you see him, or even before."

Suthiro knit his furry brown eyebrows in puzzlement, glanced for the most fleeting instant upward.

Gersen continued. "There is a stick-tight watching us, although I have not located it. Its microphone probably registers our conversation. Until you told me, I had no idea that the Star King at Smade's Tavern was Malagate. I am interested. I do not think this is common knowledge."

"Quiet!" hissed Suthiro, eyes blazing with sudden red wrath.

Gersen lowered his voice. "Hildemar Dasce quite possibly will be asked to punish you. If you wish to forestall Godogma, if you wish to take your wagon across Gorobundur Steppe —kill Dasce and go."

Suthiro hissed something below his breath, jerked up his hand as if to throw, then backed away, turned, melted into the crowd.

Pallis relaxed, slumped into her chair. In an uncertain voice she said, "I'm not as adventurous as I supposed myself."

"I'm sorry," said Gersen, genuinely contrite. "I should never have asked you out."

"No, no. I just can't accustom myself to that kind of talk, here on the esplanade, in peaceful Avente. But I suppose I'm actually enjoying it. If you're not a criminal, who or what are you?"

"Kirth Gersen."

"You must work for the IPCC."

"No."

"Then you must be on the Institute's Special Committee."

"I'm just Kirth Gersen, private individual." He rose to his feet. "Let's walk for a bit."

They went north along the esplanade. To the left lay dark sea; to the right the edifices glowing in various soft colors; and beyond, the skyline of Avente: luminous spires against the black Alphanor night.

Pallis presently took Gersen's arm. "Tell me, what if Malagate is a Star King? What does that mean?"

"I've been wondering myself." Indeed, Gersen had been trying to remember the look of the Star King. Had it been Warweave? Kelle? Or Detteras? The lusterless black skin tone had blurred the features; the striped coif had covered the hair. Gersen had an impression that the Star King had been taller than Kelle, but not quite so tall as Warweave. But would even the black skin tone have camouflaged Detteras' rude rough features?

Pallis was speaking: "Will they really kill that man?"

Gersen glanced up to see if he could locate the stick-tight, without success. "I don't know. He's useful. Incidentally. . . ." Gersen hesitated, wondering anew as to the ethics of involving Pallis in the sordid affair, if only remotely.

"Incidentally what?"

"Nothing." For fear of the stick-tight's microphone Gersen dare not inquire as to the movements of Kelle, Detteras and Warweave; Malagate so far had no reason to suspect his interest.

Pallis said in an injured voice, "I still don't understand how all of this affects you."

Once more Gersen chose to be discreet. The stick-tight might hear; Pallis Atwrode herself might be an agent of Malagate's, though Gersen considered this unlikely. So he said, "Not at all—except in the abstract."

"But any of these people—" she nodded at the passersby "—they might be Star Kings. How could we separate them from men?"

"It's hard. On their home planet—I won't attempt to

pronounce it—they come in many approximations to man. Those who travel the known worlds as observers—spies, if you prefer, although I can't imagine what they hope to learn—they're almost exact facsimiles of true men."

Pallis suddenly seemed subdued. She opened her mouth to speak, then closed it again, and finally gave a gay fling of her hands. "Let's forget about them. Nightmares. You have me seeing Star Kings everywhere. Even at the university. . . ."

Gersen looked down into her upturned face. "Do you know what I'd like to do?"

She smiled provocatively. "No. What?"

"First I'd like to shake off the stick-tight, which is no great problem. And then. . . ."

"And then?"

"I'd like to go somewhere quiet, where we could be alone."

She looked away. "I don't mind. There's a place down the coast. Les Sirenes, it's called. I've never been there." She laughed in embarrassment. "But I've heard people talking."

Gersen took her arm. "First to shake off the stick-tight. . . ."

Pallis entered into the maneuvers with childlike abandon. Looking into the merry face, Gersen wondered about his resolve to avoid emotional involvements. If they went to Les Sirenes, if the night brought them to closer intimacy, what then? Gersen thrust aside his qualms. He could cope with problems as they arose.

The stick-tight, if it had existed, was confounded and lost; they returned to the parking area. There was little light; the ranked round shapes glimmered with silky dull highlights.

They came to the slide car; Gersen hesitated, then put his arms around the swaying girl, kissed her upturned face.

Behind him was the loom of movement; ahead a furtive shifting. Gersen turned, in time to look into a horrid blood-red face with poisonous blue cheeks. Hildemar Dasce's arm descended; a great weight curled over Gersen's head; lightning exploded inside his skull. He tottered and fell to his knees. Dasce leaned over him. Gersen tried to dodge. The world reeled and toppled; he saw Suthiro grinning like a sick hyena, with his hand to the girls' neck. Dasce struck again, and the world went dim. Gersen had time for an instant of bitter self-reproach, before another thunderous buffet extinguished his consciousness.

99

Chapter 9

Excerpt from "When Is a Man Not a Man," by Podd Hachinsky, article in *Cosmopolis*, June, 1500:

...As men have traveled from star to star they have encountered many forms of life, intelligent and nonintelligent (to emphasize a perfectly arbitrary and possibly anthropomorphic parameter). No more than half a dozen of these life forms merit the adjective "humanoid." Of these half dozen, a single species closely resembles man: the Star Kings of Ghnarumen.

Ever since our initial astounded contact with the race, the question has recurred: Are they of the family of man—the "bifurcate, bibrachiate, monocephaloid, polygamite," as Tallier Chantron waggishly puts it—or are they not? The answer, of course, depends on definitions.

One point can instantly be settled: the Star Kings are not *homo sapiens*. But if what is meant is a creature which can talk a human language, walk into a haberdashery and dress himself off a rack, play an excellent game of tennis, or fight a bout of chess, attend the regal functions of Stockholm or the lawn fêtes of Strylvania without occasioning a lift of autocratic eyebrow—then that creature is a man.

Man or not man, the typical Star King is a courteous, even-tempered fellow, even if suspicious and humorless. Do him a favor and he will thank you, but feel no obligation; injure him and he will explode in tigerish fury and kill you—if he is in a situation where human law cannot restrain him. If such action will cause legal trouble, he will instantly dismiss the injury and hold no grudge. He is ruthless but not cruel, and is puzzled by such perverse human manifestations as sadism, masochism, religious fervor, flagellation, suicide. On the other hand, he will demonstrate a whole battery of peculiar habits and attitudes no less inexplicable from our point of view, arising from the twists and quirks of his own psyche.

To say that his origin is in dispute is like a remark to the effect that Croesus was well off. At least a dozen theories to explain the remarkable similarity between Star King and Man exist: none completely convincing. If the Star Kings themselves know, they will admit nothing. Since they bar all anthropological and archaeological research teams from their planet, we are afforded neither verification nor refutal of any of these theories.

On human planets they punctiliously model their conduct after the best human examples, but their innate behavior patterns are unique to the race. Perhaps to oversimplify, one can say that their dominant trait is a passion to excel, to outdo a competitor at his own game. Since man is the dominant creature of the Oikumene, the Star Kings accept him as a cynosure, a champion to be challenged and outdone, and so they strive to outdo man in every aspect of the human capacity. If this ambition (at which they are often successful) seems unreal and artificial to us, no less so does our sexual drive seem to them; for the Star Kings are parthenogenetic, reproducing in a manner which is beyond the scope of this article to describe. Knowing nothing of vanity, setting no store by either beauty or ugliness, they strive for physical perfection only to score points in their semi-amicable contest with true men. . . .

What of their achievements? They are fine builders, daring engineers, excellent technicians. They are a pragmatic race, not particularly apt at mathematics or the speculative sciences. It is hard to conceive of their giving birth to a Jarnell, who discovered the space splitter by sheer accident. Their cities are impressive sights, rising from the flatlands like a growth of metallic crystals. Each adult Star King builds for himself a spire or tower. The more fervent his ambition and the more exalted his rank, the higher and more splendid his tower (which he seems to enjoy only as a monument). Upon his demise the tower may be temporarily occupied by some junior individual during the period in which he accumulates sufficient wealth to build his own tower. Inspirational as the cities seem from a distance, they lack the most obvious municipal utilities, and the areas between the towers are unpaved, dusty, littered. Factories, industrial plants, and the like are housed in low utilitarian domes and manned by the least aggressive and least evolved of the species—for the race is by no means homogeneous. It is as if every human gathering included Proconsuls, Pithecanthropi, *sinanthropus giganticus*, Neanderthals, Magdalenians, Solutreans, Grimaldi, Cro-Magnon, and all the races of Modern Man.

101

*   *   *   *   *   *   *

At midnight a group of young folk came laughing and sing-ing into the parking area. They had dined with unaccustomed amplitude at The Halls; they had visited Llanfelfair, Lost Star Inn, Haluce, the Casino Plageale; they were intoxicated, but as much by exuberance as by the wines, smokes, per-fusions, subliminal whirligigs, chants, voltes and other exalt-ments purveyed by the houses which they had visited. The youth who stumbled over Gersen's body uttered first a jocu-lar malediction, then an exclamation of shocked concern. The group gathered; one ran to his vehicle, pressed the emer-gency call button; two minutes later a police craft dropped down from the sky, and shortly afterward an ambulance.

Gersen was conveyed to a hospital, where he was treated for concussion and shock with appropriate irradiation, mas-sage and vitalizing medicines. He presently returned to con-sciousness, and for a moment lay thinking. Then he gave a sudden lurch and tried to rise from the bed. The attending interns cautioned him, but Gersen, paying no heed, struggled erect and stood swaying.

"My clothes!" he croaked. "Give me my clothes!"

"They're safe in the closet, sir. Relax, recline, if you please. Here is the police officer, who will take your evidence."

Gersen lay back, sick with apprehension. The police in-vestigator approached: a keen-faced young man wearing the yellow-brown jacket and black breeches of the Sea Province Constabulary. He addressed himself to Gersen politely, seated himself, opened the flap of the recorder lens.

"Now, sir, what happened?"

"I was out for the evening with a young woman, Miss Pallis Atwrode of Remo. When we came back to the car, I was slugged, and I don't know what happened to Miss At-wrode. The last thing I remember, she was struggling to es-cape from one of the men."

"There were how many?"

"Two. I recognized them. Their names are Hildemar Dasce and a man I know only as Suthiro, a Sarkoy. Both are no-torious men Beyond."

"I see. The young lady's name and address?"

"Pallis Atwrode, Merioneth Apartments, Remo."

"We'll check at once to make sure she hasn't arrived home. Now, Mr. Gersen, let's go over this again."

In a dull voice Gersen gave a detailed account of the attack, described Hildemar Dasce and Suthiro. As he spoke, a report came in from Constabulary Control: Pallis Atwrode had not returned to her apartment. Roads, airways and space terminals were under observation. The IPCC had been called into the case.

"Now, sir," said the investigator in a neutral voice, "May I inquire your business?"

"I am a locater."

"What is the nature of your association with these two men?"

"None. I saw them at work once before, on Smade's Planet. Apparently they regard me as an enemy. I believe that they are part of Attel Malagate's organization."

"Very strange that they should commit an actionable offense so brazenly. In fact, why did they not kill you?"

"I don't know." Gersen once more staggered to his feet. The investigator watched with professional attentiveness. "What are your plans, Mr. Gersen?"

"I want to find Pallis Atwrode."

"Understandable, sir. But best that you do not interfere. The police are more effective than a single man. We should have news for you at any time."

"I don't think so," said Gersen. "By now they're in space."

The investigator, rising to his feet, made tacit admission that such was the case. "We will naturally keep you informed." He bowed, departed.

Gersen immediately dressed, with the disapproving help of an orderly. His knees were weak; his head floated in a kind of generalized all-embracing pain; there was a faint singing in his ears from the drugs.

An elevator dropped him directly to a subway station; Gersen stood on an exchange platform, straining to formulate a coherent plan of action. A phrase kept repeating itself compulsively, like an inchworm traversing the inner surface of his skull: Poor Pallis, poor Pallis.

With no better plan in mind, he stepped into a capsule and sent himself to a station under the Esplanade. He emerged, but instead of going to the car, took a seat in a brasserie and drank coffee. "By now she's in space," he told himself once more. "And it's my fault. My fault." Because he should have foreseen this sort of outcome. Pallis Atwrode knew Warweave, Kelle and Detteras well; she saw them daily, heard whatever gossip there was to be heard. Malagate the Star King, Malagate the Woe, was one of three men, and Pallis Atwrode evidently had knowledge which,

103

coupled to Suthiro's indiscretions, made Malagate's incognito insecure. Hence she must be removed. Killed? Sold into slavery? Taken by Dasce for his personal use? Poor Pallis, poor Pallis!

Gersen looked out over the ocean. A rim of lavender was forming at the horizon, presaging dawn. The stars were fading.

"I've got to face up to it," Gersen told himself. "It's my responsibility. If she is harmed—but no. I'll kill Hildemar Dasce in any event. . . ." Suthiro, treacherous, fox-faced Suthiro was already as good as dead. And there was Malagate himself, the architect of the entire evil construction. As a Star King he somehow seemed less hateful: a dire beast, which might be expunged without emotion.

Surfeited with hate and grief and misery, Gersen went to the car in the now empty parking area. There was the spot where Dasce had stood. There, where he had lain unconscious —what a wretched careless fool! How the spirit of his grandfather must writhe in shame!

He started the car, returned to his hotel. There were no messages.

Dawn had come to Avente. Rigel threw wide horizontal fans of light between the distant Catiline Hills and a darkling bank of clouds. Gersen set the alarm dial, dosed himself with a two-hour soporific, threw himself down on the bed.

He awoke to gloom and depression even more intense than before. Time had passed; whatever had been in store for Pallis Atwrode was now fact. Gersen ordered coffee; he could not bring himself to eat.

He considered what he must do. The IPCC? He would be forced to tell everything he knew. Could the IPCC act more efficiently if he laid his information before them? He could tell them that he suspected an administrator of the Sea Province University to be one of the so-called Demon Princes. What then? The IPCC, an elite police force, with the vices and virtues characteristic of such an organization, might or might not be trustworthy. Star Kings had possibly-infiltrated the group: in that case Malagate would certainly be warned. And how could the information help rescue Pallis Atwrode? Hildemar Dasce was the kidnaper; Gersen had reported this, and no information could be more explicit.

Another possibility: the exchange of Teehalt's world for Pallis Atwrode. . . . Gersen would gladly accept the trade— but whom to trade with? He still could not identify Malagate. The IPCC no doubt would have means to detect him. Then

104

what? The exchange would no longer be conceivable. There might be a quiet execution—though the IPCC generally acted only upon the formal request of some authorized governmental agency. And in the meantime, what of Pallis Atwrode? She would be lost—a small delightful spark of life extinguished, forgotten.

But if Gersen knew Malagate's identity he would have vastly more leverage. He could make his offer with assurance. The logic of the situation seemed to be that Gersen proceed as before. But how slow! Think of Pallis, poor Pallis! Nevertheless, Hildemar Dasce had gone Beyond, and no effort of Gersen or of the IPCC could avail against this hard fact. Attel Malagate alone had the power to order his return. If Pallis Atwrode still lived.

The situation had not changed. As before, his first urgency was: identify Malagate. Then: bargain, or extort.

With his course of action once more clear, Gersen's spirits lifted. More accurately, his resolve and dedication burned at a fervent new heat. Hate gave him a heady, almost drunken, sense of omnipotence. No one, nothing, could withstand emotion so intense!

The hour of his appointment with Detteras, Warweave and Kelle was approaching. Gersen dressed, descended to the garage, slid his car out upon the avenue and headed south.

Arriving at the university, he parked, rode the slideway to the mall, crossed the quadrangle to the College of Galactic Morphology. Hoping against hope, with a sudden quick jerking of the heart, he looked toward the reception desk. A different girl was on duty. He asked politely, "Where is Miss Atwrode this morning?"

"I don't know, sir. She hasn't arrived. Perhaps she's not feeling well."

Perhaps indeed, thought Gersen. He mentioned his appointment and proceeded to the office of Rundle Detteras.

Warweave and Kelle were there before him. The three undoubtedly had reached a common decision, a common course of action. Gersen looked from face to face, Detteras to Warweave to Kelle. One of these creatures was human only in similitude. At Smade's Tavern he had glimpsed him, and he tried to think back, to visualize, to remember. No image came. Black-dyed skin and exotic costume were a disguise beyond his penetration. Furtively he assessed each. Which? Warweave: aquiline, cold-eyed, arrogant? Kelle: precise, humorless, austere? Or Detteras, whose geniality now seemed insincere and counterfeit?

He could not decide. He forced himself into a pose of studious courtesy, and made his primary gambit. "Let's simplify the whole matter," said Gersen. "I'll pay you—by this I naturally mean the college—for the decoding strip. I imagine the college could use a thousand SVU. In any event, that's the offer I wish to make."

His adversaries, each in his own style, seemed taken aback. Warweave raised his brows, Kelle stared fixedly, Detteras put on a puzzled half smile.

Warweave said, "But we understood that you intended to sell what you conceived to be your interest in this matter."

"I don't mind selling," said Gersen. "If you'll offer me enough."

"And how much is enough?"

"A million SVU, perhaps two, or perhaps three, if you'll go that high."

Kelle snorted, Detteras shook his big ugly head.

"Fees of that sort are not paid to locaters," said Warweave.

"Has it been established which of you sent out Teehalt?" asked Gersen.

"What does it matter?" asked Warweave. "Your interest in the affair—money—has become clear enough." He looked from Kelle to Detteras. "Whoever it is has either forgotten or does not care to disclose himself. Doubtless that is the way the situation will remain."

Detteras said, "It's certainly inconsequential. Come now, Mr. Gersen, we have decided to make you a joint offer—certainly not as grandiose as the figure you name—"

"How much?"

"Possibly as much as 5,000 SVU."

"Ridiculous. This is an exceptional world."

"You do not know this," Warweave pointed out. "You have not been there; or so you claim."

"More to the point," said Kelle dryly, "neither have we."

"You have seen the photographs," said Gersen.

"Exactly," said Kelle. "We have seen no more. Photographs can be faked without difficulty. I for one do not propose to pay out a large sum on the strength of three photographs."

"Understandable," said Gersen. "But for my part I don't intend to make a move without a guarantee. Don't forget I have suffered a loss, and this is my opportunity to make it good."

"Be reasonable!" Detteras urged bluffly. "Without the decoder, the filament is just another spool of wire."

"Not completely. Fourier analysis eventually can break the code."

"In theory. It is a long expensive process."

"Not as expensive as giving the filament away for next to nothing."

The discussion continued for an hour, Gersen gritting his teeth in impatience. A price of 100,000 SVU, to be deposited in escrow, was eventually arranged; the sale conditional upon a list of provisos relating to the physical characteristics of the world in question.

Agreement having been reached, telescreen contact with the Bureau of Deeds and Contracts at Avente was made. The four men identified themselves formally, represented their interests; the contract was read into the records.

A second call, to the Bank of Alphanor, established the escrow account.

The three administrators now sat back and inspected Gersen, who in his turn looked from one to the other. "So much is settled. Which of you goes with me to inspect this world?"

The three exchanged glances. "I'll go," said Warweave. "I'll be very much interested to go."

"I was about to volunteer my own services," said Detteras.

"In that case," said Kelle, "I might as well come along too. I'm very much overdue for a change."

Gersen seethed in frustration. He had expected Malagate —whoever he might be—to volunteer his services; in fact, to assert them. Gersen could then take this individual aside and offer a new set of conditions: the filament for Pallis Atwrode. What, after all, was the world to him? His single goal was Malagate's identity, and after that his life.

But now this plan had gone by the boards. If all three went out to Teehalt's planet, the identification of Malagate must depend upon new circumstances. Meanwhile the fate of Pallis Atwrode bore no thinking about.

Gersen made a last-ditch protest. "My boat is small for four. Better if only one went out with me."

"No difficulty there," Detteras stated. "We will go out in the departmental ship. Plenty of room aboard."

"Another matter," said Gersen gruffly. "I have urgent business I must see to in the near future. I am sorry to inconvenience you, but I insist that we leave today."

There was vigorous and general protest: all three declared

107

themselves tied up for at least a week by engagements, appointments, and commitments.

Gersen put on a show of temper. "Gentlemen, you have wasted enough of my time. We leave today, or I'll take the filament elsewhere—or destroy it." He watched the three faces, hoping to surprise Malagate in dismay. Warweave gave him a glance of metallic dislike; Kelle examined him as if he were an insubordinate child; Detteras shook his head ruefully. There was a moment of silence. Who would be the first to agree, no matter how reluctantly, to the conditions?

Warweave said in a colorless voice, "I consider that you are taking a very arbitrary and high-handed position."

"Confound it," grumbled Detteras, "I can't simply ditch everything in five minutes."

"One of you should be able to tear yourself loose," Gersen suggested hopefully. "We can make a preliminary survey—sufficient so I can take my money and be off about my business."

"Humph," grunted Detteras.

Kelle said slowly, "I suppose that I would be able to go out."

Warweave nodded. "My engagements, with considerable inconvenience, can be postponed."

Detteras threw his hands into the air, turned to the screen, called his secretary. "Cancel all my appointments. Urgent business is taking me out of town."

"For how long, sir?"

"I don't know," said Detteras, with a hard glance for Gersen. "Indefinitely."

Gersen continued his inspection of the three men. Detteras alone had displayed irritation. Kelle obviously regarded the trip as an unexpected outing; Warweave maintained a cool detachment.

So much for that particular ploy, thought Gersen. He went to stand by the door. "We'll meet at the spaceport, agreed? At—let us say—seven o'clock. I will bring the filament; one of you must bring the decoding strip."

The three acquiesced, and Gersen departed.

Returning to Avente, Gersen pondered the future. What challenges would he face from these three men, one of whom was Attel Malagate? It would be foolhardy not to make preparations, to arrange safeguards: this was the training imposed upon him by his grandfather, a methodical man, who had labored diligently to discipline Gersen's innate tendency to rely upon improvisation.

At the hotel Gersen examined his belongings, and made certain selections; then packed and checked out. After painstaking precautions against stick-tights and human trackers, he went to a branch office of the Amalgamated Distribution Service, another of the monster semipublic utility companies with agencies throughout the Oikumene. In a booth he consulted catalogues which offered him a choice of a million products produced by thousands of fabricators. Making his choice, he punched the requisite buttons, went to the service counter.

There was a wait of three minutes, while automatic machinery ranged the shelves of the enormous underground warehouse; then the mechanism Gersen had ordered appeared on a belt. He examined it, paid the clerk, departed, and rode the subway to the spaceport. He inquired the location of the university ship from an attendant, who took him out on a terrace and pointed down the long line of spacecraft large and small, each in its bay.

"Notice, sir, the red and yellow yacht with side platform? Well, count down three. First the CD 16, then the old Parabola, and then the green and blue ship with the big observation dome. That's the job. She's going out today, eh?"

"Yes. About seven. How did you know?"

"One of the crew is already aboard. I had to let him on."

"I see." Gersen went down to the field, walked along the way which led past the ranked spacecraft. From the shadow of the ship in the next bay, he inspected the university ship. The contours were distinctive, as was the rather elaborate emblem at the bow. Recollection stirred at the back of his mind: somewhere before he had seen this ship. Where? At Smade's Planet on the landing field between mountains and black ocean. It was the ship used by the Star King.

The shape of a man passed in front of one of the observation windows. When he moved out of sight Gersen crossed the space between the two ships.

Cautiously he tried the outer entry port; it eased ajar. He stepped into the transition chamber, peered through the panel into the ship's main saloon. Suthiro the Sarkoy worked at an object which he apparently had attached to the underside of a shelf.

Inside Gersen something more ferocious than gladness— a peculiar exaltation of hate—swelled and burst, suffusing his entire body. He tried the inner portal; it was locked from within. There was, however, an emergency disengagement which would unlock the door if pressure were equalized between cabin and outer atmosphere. Gersen touched the emergency switch. There was an audible click. Within the ship, all was silent. Not daring to glance through the panel, Gersen pressed his ear to the port. Useless: no sound could pass through the laminated structure. He waited a minute, then carefully eased himself up to look into the cabin once more.

Suthiro had heard nothing. He had gone forward, and now appeared to be adjusting the padding around a stanchion. His heavy flat-skulled head was bent forward, his lips were pursed out.

Gersen slid back the port and stepped into the cabin, a projac pointed at the big square buckle of Suthiro's stepperider harness. "Skop Suthiro," said Gersen. "This is a pleasure for which I had not dared hope."

Suthiro's dog-brown eyes opened and shut; he grinned broadly. "I was waiting for your arrival."

"Indeed. And why?"

"I wanted to continue our discussion of last night."

"We were speaking of Godogma, the long-legged walker with wheels on his feet. Plainly he has wheeled across the path of your life, and you will never drive your wagon over the Gorobundur."

Suthiro became very still, his eyes measuring Gersen.

"What happened to the girl?" asked Gersen gently.

Suthiro considered, then rejected the feasibility of feigning innocence. "She was taken by Fancy Dasce."

"With your connivance. Where is she now?"

Suthiro shrugged. "He had orders to kill her. Why, I don't know. I am told very little. Dasce will not kill her. Not till he has the full use of her. He is a *khet*." Suthiro sneered the epithet, a metaphor linking Dasce to the obscenely fecund Sarkovy mink.

"He has left Alphanor?"

"Certainly." Suthiro seemed surprised at Gersen's naiveté. "Probably for his little planet." He made a fretful uncomfortable motion, which brought him an imperceptible four inches closer to Gersen.

"Where is this planet?"

"Ha! Do you think he would tell me? Or anyone else?"

"In that case—but I must ask you to stand back."

"Pah," whispered Suthiro in a childish display of petulance. "I can poison you any time I choose."

Gersen allowed a faint smile to cross his lips. "I have already poisoned you."

110

Suthiro raised his eyebrows. "When? You have never closed with me."

"Last night. I touched you when I handed you paper. Look at the back of your right hand."

Suthiro stared in slow horror at the red weal. "Cluthe!" Gersen nodded. "Cluthe."

"But—why should you do this to me?"

"You merit such an end."

Suthiro launched himself like a leopard; the projector in Gersen's hand discharged a stalk of blue-white energy. Suthiro fell to the deck, lay staring up at Gersen. "Better plasma than cluthe," he whispered huskily.

"You'll die by cluthe," said Gersen.

Suthiro shook his head. "Not while I carry my poisons."

"Godogma calls you. So now speak truth. Do you hate Hildemar Dasce?"

"I hate Dasce indeed." Suthiro seemed surprised, as if there were anyone who did not hate Dasce.

"I would kill Dasce."

"Most people would do no less."

"Where is his planet?"

"Beyond. I know no more."

"When are you to see him next?"

"Never. I am dying, and Dasce is bound for a deeper hell than mine."

"If you lived?"

"Never. I was to return to Sarkovy."

"Who knows of this planet?"

"Malagate . . . perhaps."

"Is there no one else? Tristano?"

"No. Dasce tells little. The world is airless." Suthiro carefully hunched himself together. "Already the skin begins to itch."

"Listen, Suthiro. You hate Dasce. Yes? And you hate me, for I have poisoned you. Think! You, a Sarkoy, poisoned by me, and so easily."

Suthiro muttered, "I hate you indeed."

"Tell me how to find Dasce, then. One of us must kill the other. The death will be your doing."

Suthiro rocked his furry head in desolation. "But I cannot tell you what I do not know."

"What has he said of his world? Does he talk?"

"He boasts: Dasce is a vile braggart. His world is harsh; only a man like himself could master this world. He lives in the crater of a dead volcano."

111

"What of the sun?"

Suthiro hunched himself together. "It is dim. Yes. It must be red. They asked Dasce about his face—in a tavern. Why had he dyed himself red? To match his sun, said Dasce, which was the same color, and not much larger.

"A red dwarf," mused Gersen.

"So it might be."

"Think! What else? Which direction? Which constellation? Which sector?"

"He says nothing. And now—I do not care. I think only of Godogma. Go away so that I may kill myself decently."

Gersen surveyed the huddled form without emotion. "What are you doing here in the ship?"

Suthiro looked at his hand curiously, then rubbed his chest. "I feel it moving." He examined Gersen. "Well, then, since you would look on my death: watch." He put hands to his neck, convulsed his knuckles. The brown eyes stared. "In thirty seconds now."

"Who would know of Dasce's planet? Has he friends?"

"Friends?" Suthiro, even in his last seconds, took occasion to sneer.

"Where does he lodge in Avente?"

"North of Sailmaker Beach. In an old hut on Melnoy Heights."

"Who is Malagate? What is his name?"

Suthiro spoke in a whisper. "A Star King has no name."

"What name does he use on Alphanor?"

The thick lips opened and closed. Words rattled in the pale throat. "You killed me. Should Dasce fail, let Malagate kill you." The eylids jerked, quivered. Suthiro lay back, seemed to stiffen, made no further movement.

Gersen looked down at the body. He walked around behind it, studied it. The Sarkoy were notoriously treacherous and revengeful. With his toe he attempted to turn the body over on its face. Quick as the strike of a serpent the arm flashed around, poison prongs ready. Gersen jerked back; the projac ejected a second dazzling line of energy. This time Suthiro the Sarkoy lay truly dead.

Gersen searched the corpse. In the pouch he found a sum of money, which he tucked into his own wallet. There was a kit of poisons, which Gersen examined, then, unable to comprehend Suthiro's cryptic nomenclature, discarded; also a device no larger than his thumb, intended to project crystalline needles of poison or virus on a jet of compressed air: a man could be infected from a distance of fifty feet

112

and know nothing save a faint tingle. Suthiro carried a projac similar to his own, three stilettos, a packet of fruit lozenges, undoubtedly lethal.

Gersen dropped the weapons back into Suthiro's pouch, dragged the body to a waste ejection locker, and crammed it away out of sight. Once in space, the touch of a button would dispose of Sivij Suthiro the Sarkoy. Next he looked to discover what Suthiro, while alive, had so earnestly been trying to achieve. Under the shelf he found a small toggle switch controlling a set of wires which led to a concealed relay, which in turn activated the valves on four reservoirs of gas at various secret spots around the cabin. Death gas or anaesthetic? He detached one of the reservoirs and found a label printed in the crabbed Sarkoy syllabary: *Tironvirasko's Instantaneous Narcoleptic; an odorless sleep inducent with minimal post reducts*. It seemed that Malagate, no less methodical than Gersen, was taking his own precautions.

Gersen took each of the four reservoirs to the entry port, released their contents, replaced them where he had found them. He left Suthiro's switch in place, but changed its function.

This accomplished, Gersen brought out his own device: the timer he had purchased at Amalgamated, and a grenade from his armament.

After a moment's reflection, he secured it inside the reactor housing, where it would do maximum damage, and yet be convenient in case of need.

He glanced at his watch: one o'clock. Time was growing short. Far too short to accomplish all that must be done. He departed, locking the ship behind him and, returning to the terminal, took the subway for Sailmaker Beach.

At a stand beside the station Gersen selected a self-service cab—a single-seat scooter, gyroscopically balanced, with a transparent canopy. Two SVU in the slot gave him possession for an hour. Stepping aboard, he drove north through the noisy streets of Sailmaker Beach.

The district had a unique flavor. Avente, a suave cosmopolitan city, was almost indistinguishable from fifty other polities of the Oikumene. Sailmaker Beach resembled no other locale in the known universe. The buildings were low, thick-walled, constructed for the most part of crushed coquina concrete, white or color-washed; in the blazing light of Rigel even pastels seemed intense. For some reason lavender and pale blue, along with white, were the most popular tints. The district was home to scores of off-world nationalities, each forming an enclave, each with its characteristic food shops, restaurants, specialty houses. Though widely disparate of origin, habit and physiognomy, the inhabitants of the district were uniformly voluble, half suspicious, half naive, contemptuous of outsiders, equally contemptuous of each other. They earned their living from tourists, as domestic servants or day laborers, as proprietors of small shops and craft studios, as entertainers or musicians in the innumerable taverns, bistros, bordellos, restaurants.

At the north rose Melnoy Heights, and here the architecture changed to tall narrow apartment buildings, of almost Gothic elongation, each seeming to peer over the other's shoulder, across Sailmaker Beach to the more conventional districts. In Melnoy Heights Hildemar Dasce reputedly had lodgings. As methodically as shortness of time and anxiety allowed, Gersen sought information regarding him.

There was no Hildemar Dasce listed in the Melnoy Heights Directory—nor had Gersen expected to find one. Dasce undoubtedly would desire privacy, the pose of normality.

Gersen began to visit the taverns, describing the tall man with the split nose, the red skin, the chalk-blue cheeks. He soon encountered folk who had noticed Dasce, but not until the fourth tavern did he find anyone who had spoken with him.

"You must mean Beauty," said the bartender, a stubby orange-skinned man, with russet hair arranged in fine glossy festoons and curls. Gersen stared in fascination at the chain carved from turquoise which looped from a hole in his left nostril to a hole in the lobe of his left ear. "Beauty comes in often to drink. A spaceman, he claims himself, but as to this I can't be certain. I have often declared myself a great lover. All of us lie, as much or more than necessary. 'What is truth?' asks Pons Pilatus, in the fable, and I answer: 'A commodity as cheap as air which we hide as if it were as precious as yewl stone.'" The bartender was disposed to further philosophy; Gersen hauled him back to the issue at hand. "Where does Beauty Dasce house himself?"

"Up the hill, up back." The bartender made a vague gesture. "I can tell you no more, because I know no more."

Gersen rode his scooter up the steep lanes and switchbacks of Melnoy Heights. Inquiry at another tavern, a tiresome series of questions at various shops, lobbies and street corners, finally resulted in explicit directions to Dasce's lodgings. Riding a little unpaved road which left the area of tall apartments, Gersen circled a steep rocky hillside, where gangs of children scrambled like goats. At the end of the road stood an isolated rectangular cottage, rudely, if substantially, constructed. It commanded a magnificent view over the ocean; over Sailmaker Beach; the Grand Esplanade, dwindling far to the south; and, only just perceptible through the haze, the apartment towers of Remo.

Gersen approached the cottage with care, though it exuded the indefinable but unmistakable feeling of vacancy. He walked around peering through the windows, seeing nothing of interest. After a quick glance to right and left, he broke in the sash of an inconspicuous window, and cautiously, in the event that Dasce had set out mantraps, climbed into the cottage.

The house was strong with the feel of Dasce's habitancy: a faintly acrid odor, together with an aura more subtle than odor, of crudeness, dark, pompous, magnificent strength. There were four rooms, encompassing the usual functions. Gersen made a quick general investigation, then concentrated his attention upon the parlor. The ceiling was scrolled plaster, painted pale yellow. The floor was covered by a carpet of greenish-yellow fiber, the walls were a checkerboard of maroon and dark brown hardwood tiles. At the far end Dasce had placed a desk and a heavy chair. The wall over the desk was hung with dozens of photographs: Dasce in all poses, against every variety of background.

There was Dasce in startling close-up, revealing every pore of his skin, the split cartilage of his nose, the lidless blue eyes. There was Dasce in the costume of a Bernal flame fighter—varnished black plates and horns and cusps and prongs, like a titanic stag beetle. There was Dasce in a palanquin of yellow rattan, hung with persimmon silk, borne on the shoulders of six black-haired maidens. The angle of the wall displayed a set of photographs of a man who was not Dasce. Apparently they had been taken over a period of years. The first showed the face of a man thirty years old: a sturdy, confident, bulldog face, serene, even complacent. The face had changed alarmingly in the second of the photographs. The cheeks were sunken, the eyes started from their sockets, the nerves at the temples showed in an intricate mesh. In each succeeding photograph the face became ever more haggard. . . . Gersen glanced along a row of books: pornography of a childishly obscene nature, weapon manuals, an index to Sarkoy poisons, a late edition of *Handbook to*

115

the Planets, an index to Dasce's microbook library, a *Star Directory.*

The desk itself was extremely handsome: side panels of dark wood carved to represent griffins and winged serpents in a jungle; the surface an exquisite inlay of opals polished flat. Gersen checked the drawers and pigeonholes. They were barren of information—completely empty, in fact. Gersen stood back, a tide of grim despair rising within him. He looked at his watch. In four hours he must meet Detteras, Warweave and Kelle at the spaceport. He stood in the center of the room, carefully scrutinized every article. Somewhere must be a link with Dasce's secret planet; how to recognize it?

He went to the book shelf, took down the *Star Directory,* examined the lay of the binding. If Dasce's red dwarf were listed he certainly must have located it in the directory. If he had done so several times, there might be a crease, a smear, a discoloration. No such mark was visible. Gersen held the book by its two covers, let it hang. A third through the book the pages separated a hairbreadth. Gersen carefully opened the book at this spot, looked down the listing. Each star—and on this page there were two hundred—was described under eleven headings: index number, constellation placement as viewed from Earth, star type, planetary information, mass, vector of velocity, diameter, density, location coordinates, distance from the center of the Oikumene, remarks.

Twenty-three red dwarfs were listed. Eight of these were double. Eleven hung solitary in space, forlorn feeble sparks. Four were accompanied by planets, eight planets in all. These four Gersen scrutinized with especial care. Reluctantly he was forced to conclude that none of these planets could conceivably be considered habitable. Five of the planets were too hot, one was completely awash in liquid methane, two were too massive to allow human toleration of the gravity. Gersen's mouth drooped in disappointment. Nothing. Still, the page at one time had been earnestly consulted; there must be information here which Dasce needed or valued. Gersen tore the page from the book.

The front door opened; Gersen whirled. In the opening stood a middle-aged man no larger than a boy of ten. His head was round; his eyes brimmed with curiosity, flicking over Gersen, around the room. He had large features, long pointed ears, a heavy protuberant mouth: a Highland Imp from the Highlands of Krokinole, one of the more specialized races of the Concourse.

He came forward, fearlessly swaggering. "Who are you, that's in Mr. Spock's house? Looking through Mr. Spock's things? A burglar, I think."

Gersen replaced the book, and the Imp said, "That's one of his precious volumes, that bit of stuff. Not likely he wants your fingers all over it. I'd better go for the constable."

"Come back here," said Gersen. "Who are you?"

"I'm the by-your-leave caretaker, that's who I am. Also this is my land and my house and my freehold. Mr. Spock is the man I let to, and why should I give every burglar north of Swansea leave to pillage and loot?"

"Mr. Spock is a criminal," said Gersen.

"And if he is, it's proof then that there's no honor among thieves."

"I'm no thief," said Gersen mildly. "The IPCC is after your tenant, Mr. Spock."

The Imp bent his big head forward. "Be you IPCC? Show me your blazer."

On the assumption that a Krokinole Imp would not recognize an IPCC blazer when he saw one, Gersen displayed a transparent tablet, with his photograph under a gold seven-pointed star. He touched it to his forehead and it glowed into light, a factitious display which impressed the Imp. He instantly became effusive in his cordiality.

"Never did think that Mr. Spock was up to good. He'll come to a bad end, mark my words! What's he done now?"

"Kidnap. Murder."

"Bad deeds, both. I'll have to caution Mr. Spock."

"He is a wicked man. How long has he lived here?"

"Donkey's years."

"You know him well, then?"

"Well indeed. Who drinks with him when everyone else turns their heads as if Mr. Spock smelt poorly? Me. I drink with him, and frequently. It's no treat to look like Mr. Spock, and I have my compassion."

"So you're Spock's friend."

The big features twisted and moved in successive displays of tolerance, crafty speculation, virtuous indignation. "I? Certainly not. Do I look the sort who consorts with criminals?"

"But—let us say—you have heard Spock talking."

"That I have, and oh, the tales he tells!" The Imp's eyes rolled ludicrously upward. "Do I believe him? No."

"Has he ever spoken of a secret world where he has a hideaway?"

"Again and again. He calls it Thumbnail Gulch. Why? He always shakes his head when he's asked. A tight-mouthed man, Mr. Spock, for all his loose braggadocio."

"What more has he said of his world?"

The Imp shrugged. "The sun's blood-red, hardly enough to keep him warm."

"And where is this world?"

"Aha! That's where he's sly. No word of this will he speak. Many's the time I've wondered, thinking that suppose poor Mr. Spock took sick on this lonesome world—who'd know to tell his friends?"

Gersen smiled grimly. "And this argument never induced him to confide in you?"

"Never. Why do you wish to know?"

"He's kidnaped an innocent young woman and taken her to this world."

"The rogue. What a raffish creature." The Imp shook his head in distress, from which a certain measure of wistful envy was not absent. "I'll never let my land and house to him again."

"Think. What has Spock said regarding the world?"

The Imp screwed up his eyes. "Thumbnail Gulch. The world is bigger than the sun. Astonishing, no?"

"If the sun is a red dwarf, not too astonishing."

"Volcanos. There are live volcanos on this world."

"Volcanos? That's odd. A red dwarf's planet shouldn't have volcanos. It's too old."

"Old or young, the volcanos thrive. Mr. Spock lives in a dead crater, and he sees a whole line of volcanos smoking up along the horizon.

"What else?"

"Nought."

"How long does it take to get to his planet?"

"That I can't say."

"You've never met any of his friends?"

"Tosspots at the tavern, no more. But yes. One. Less than a year ago—an Earthman, a heavy cruel man."

"Tristano?"

"I know nothing of his name. Mr. Spock had just returned from a business trip Beyond, to a planet called New Hope. Do you know it?"

"I've never been there."

"Nor I, though I've wandered far. But the very day of

his return, while we sit in Gelperino's Saloon, the Earthman comes in. 'Where have you been?' he asks. 'Ten days I've been here, and we left New Hope together.' Mr. Spock gives him his haughty look. 'If you must know, I looked in on my little hideaway for half a day. I have obligations there, you know! And the Earthman said no more."

Gersen thought a moment and suddenly was in a hurry to leave. "What more do you know?"

"Nothing more."

Gersen made a last survey of the house, under the inquisitive scrutiny of the Imp, then departed, ignoring the Imp's sudden harsh demands for damages when he discovered the broken window sash. Hastily, now, Gersen rode down through the winding avenues, across Sailmaker Beach, back into central Avente. He went to an office of the Universal Technical Consultative Service, and gained the attention of an operator.

"Set up this problem," said Gersen. "Two ships leave the planet New Hope. One proceeds directly here, to Avente. The other goes to a red dwarf star, spends half a day, then comes to Avente, arriving ten days later. I want a list of the red dwarf stars which this second ship might have visited."

The operator considered. "There is obviously an ellipsoid shell here, the foci being New Hope and Alphanor. We must take into account the accelerations and decelerations, the probable coast periods and landing times. There will necessarily be a locus of most probability, and areas of diminishing probability."

"Set up the problem so that the machine lists these stars in order of probability."

"To what limits?"

"Oh—one chance in fifty. Include also the constants of these stars as given in the directory."

"Very well, sir. The fee will be 25 SVU."

Gersen brought forth money; the operator translated the problem into precise language, spoke into a microphone. Thirty seconds later a sheet of paper dropped from a slot. The operator glanced at it, signed his name, handed it without a word to Gersen.

Forty-three stars were listed. Gersen compared the list with the page he had torn from Dasce's *Directory*. A single star occurred on both lists. Gersen frowned in puzzlement. The star was a member of a binary, without planets. The couple was.... Naturally! thought Gersen, illumination flooding his mind. How else could volcanos exist on the companion of a red dwarf? Dasce's world was not a planet, but a dark star:

a dead surface, perhaps still faintly warm. Gersen had heard of such worlds. Usually they were too dense, too massive for human occupancy, but if a small star in the course of two or three billion years happened to sweep up enough detritus to build a thick shell of light material, the surface gravity might well be reduced to a tolerable level.

* * * * * * *

At ten minutes to seven, Kelle, Warweave and Detteras appeared at the spaceport, wearing spacemen's harness, their skins washed the blue-brown tone which originally, in popular credence, was thought to protect the human organism from certain mysterious Jarnell effluviae, and which by usage had become a normal adjunct to the space traveler's accoutrements. They halted in the middle of the lobby, looked about, spied Gersen, turned to face him as he approached.

Gersen surveyed them with a dour smile. "We seem to be ready, all of us. I thank you gentlemen for your promptness."

"Achieved, necessarily, at great inconvenience to all of us," stated Kelle.

"In due course the reason for haste will become clear," said Gersen. "Your luggage?"

"On its way to the ship," said Detteras.

"Then we will leave. We have clearance?"

"Everything has been arranged," said Warweave.

The group proceeded from the lobby and walked around to the docking area, toward which a crane was already trundling.

The luggage, four large cases and as many smaller packets, was stacked beside the ship. Warweave unlocked the entry ports; Gersen and Kelle passed the cases into the cabin. Detteras made a bluff attempt to assert command. "We have four compartments aboard. I'll take forward starboard; Kelle, you'll have starboard aft; Warweave, port forward; Gersen, port aft. We might as well move our luggage out of the cabin."

"One moment," said Gersen. "There is a situation that we must resolve before we proceed any further."

Detteras' big face creased in a scowl. "What sort of situation?"

"We are two parties of interest here—at least two parties. Neither trusts the other. We are going Beyond, past the edge of law. All of us, recognizing this fact, have brought

120

weapons. I propose that we lock all weapons in the security cabinet; that we open the luggage and, if necessary, strip ourselves naked, to assure each other that all the weapons have been declared. Since you are three to my one, if any advantage lies to either side, it is to yours."

"A highly undignified process," grumbled Detteras.

Kelle, more equable now than Gersen could have believed, said, "Come now, Rundle. Gersen is merely verbalizing reality. In short, I agree with him. The more so since I carry no weapons."

Warweave made a careless gesture. "Search me, search my luggage; but let's get under way."

Detteras shook his head, opened his case, withdrew a projac of great power, tossed it upon the table. "I have my doubts about the wisdom of this. I have nothing against Mr. Gersen personally—but suppose he takes us to a far planet where he has accomplices waiting, who capture us and hold us for ransom? Stranger crimes have occurred."

Gersen laughed. "If you consider this a real danger you need only remain here. I don't care whether one goes or all go."

"What of your own weapons?" asked Warweave dryly.

Gersen brought forth his projac, a pair of stilettos, a dagger, four grenades the size of walnuts.

"My word," said Detteras. "You maintain quite an armament."

"I occasionally have need for it," said Gersen. "Now, the luggage...." The accumulated arms were placed in a cabinet which was secured with four locks, each man retaining a key to one of the locks.

The crane trundled up to the ship; the boom swung around. Hooks engaged in trammels; the ship jerked, hung free, was carried out on the field.

Detteras went to the main console and touched a button, which flashed a row of green lights. "Everything ready to go," he said. "Tanks full, machinery in order."

Kelle cleared his throat and brought forth a handsomely mounted wooden case bound in red leather. "This is one of the departmental rationalizers. You have Mr. Teehalt's filament, I assume?"

"Yes," said Gersen. "I have the filament with me. But there is no hurry. Before we engage the monitor we must reach zero base point, which is far distant."

"Very well," said Detteras. "What are the coordinates?"

Gersen brought forward a slip of paper. "If you will allow

me," he said politely, "I will make the settings on the auto-pilot."

With ill grace Detteras rose to his feet. "It seems to me that there is no longer reason for distrust. We have stripped ourselves of our weapons; all the issues have been settled. So let us all relax and behave amicably."

"With pleasure," said Gersen.

The ship was lowered to the launching pad, the crane disengaged and rolled away. The group settled themselves into take-off seats; Detteras started the automatic launching sequence. There was a jar, a sense of acceleration, and Alphanor retreated below.

Chapter 10

From the chapter "Malagate the Woe," in the book *The Demon Princes*, by Caril Carphen, published by Elucidarian Press, New Wexford, Aloysius, Vega:

...In our cursory summary we have seen how each Demon Prince is unique and highly individuated, each displaying his characteristic style.

This is all the more remarkable in that the basic variety of possible crimes is limited and can be numbered on the fingers. There is crime for gain: extortion, robbery (which includes piracy and raids on settled communities), swindling in its infinite guises. There is slavery, with its various manifestations: procuring, selling, and using slaves. Murder, coercion, and torture are merely adjuncts to these activities. The personal depravities are equally limited, and can be classified under sexual debauchery, sadism, violent acts prompted by pique, vindictiveness, revenge, or vandalism.

Doubtless the catalogue is incomplete, perhaps even illogical, but this is beside the point. I merely wish to display the basic paucity, in order to illustrate this point: that each of the Demon Princes, in inflicting one or another atrocity, impresses the act with his own style and seems to create a new crime.

In the previous chapters we have examined the maniacal Kokor Hekkus and his theories of absolute frightfulness; the devious Viole Falushe, voluptuary, sybarite, and amateur of kinaesthetics.

Completely distinctive is Attel Malagate, the Woe, in style and mannerism. Rather than enlarging himself, projecting a macroscopic delineation of his person and deeds, to mesmerize his victims and intimidate his enemies, Malagate prefers the possibly equally chilling device of silence, invisibility, dispassionate impersonality. There is no reliable description of Malagate. Certainly Malagate is a cognomen, derived from a folk epic of old Quantique. He acts with implacable viciousness, although his cruelties are never wanton, and, if he maintains a pleasure palace after the style of Viole Falushe or Howard Alan Treesong, it is a well-guarded secret.

Malagate's activities are primarily extortion and slavery. In the Conclave of 1500 at Smade's Planet, where five Demon Princes and a score of lesser operators met to define and circumscribe their activities, Malagate was allotted that sector of the Beyond centered on Ferrier's Cluster. It includes over a hundred settlements, towns and vicinities, upon all of which Malagate levies assessments. He rarely encounters protest or complaint, for he need merely cite the example of Mount Pleasant, a town of 5,000 persons, which declined to meet his demands. In the year 1499 Malagate invited four other princes to join him. The junta swept down upon the town, captured and enslaved the entire population.

On the planet Grabhorne he maintains a plantation of about ten thousand square miles, with a slave population estimated at twenty thousand. Here are carefully tilled farms, and factories which build exquisite furniture, musical instruments and electronic mechanisms. The slaves are not overtly ill treated, but working hours are long, the dormitories are drab, social opportunities are restricted. Punishment is a term in the mines, which few survive.

Attel Malagate's attention is usually wide and dispassionate, but he sometimes focuses upon some individual. The planet Caro lies in an area which none of the Demon Princes claim. Mayor Janous Paragiglia of the city Desde espoused and advocated a militia and space navy sufficient to protect Caro, and to seek out and destroy Malagate or any other of the Demon Princes who dared to attack Caro. Malagate kidnaped Janous Paragiglia and tortured him for thirty-nine days, telecasting the entire process to the cities of Caro, to all the planets in his own sector, and, in one of his rare acts of bravado, to the Rigel Concourse.

As mentioned, his personal appetites are unknown. A rumor frequently encountered runs to the effect that Malagate enjoys engaging in personal gladiatorial duels with able-bodied enemies, with swords for weapons. Malagate is said to exhibit superhuman strength and dexterity, and seems to derive satisfaction from slowly hewing his opponent to bits.

Like certain other Demon Princes, Malagate maintains a discrete and respectable identity within the Oikumene and, if whispers are correct, occupies a prestigious position on one of the major worlds. . . .

* * * * * * *

Alphanor became a misty pale disk, mingled with the stars. Within the ship the four men settled into an uneasy accommodation. Kelle and Warweave started a quiet conversation. Detteras stared forward into star-spattered emptiness. Gersen lounged to the side, watching the three men.

One of them—not completely a man, or better, a simulated man—was Malagate the Woe. Which?

Gersen thought he knew.

There was still no certainty in his mind; his conjecture was based on indications, probabilities, suppositions. Malagate, for his part, must still feel secure in his incognito. He had no reason to suspect Gersen's objective; he must still consider Gersen no more than an aquisitive locater out to drive as hard a bargain as he could. So much the better, thought Garsen, if it would help him to a sure identification. He wanted two things only: the freedom of Pallis Atwrode, and the death of Malagate. And, of course, of Hildemar Dasce. If Pallis Atwrode were dead—so much the worse for Dasce.

Surreptitiously Gersen watched his suspect. Was this man Malagate? Frustrating to be so close to his goal. Malagate, of course, had his own plans. Behind the human skull worked thought patterns incommensurable to his own, moving toward a goal still obscure.

Gersen could define at least three areas of uncertainty in the situation. First, did Malagate still carry weapons or have access to weapons previously concealed aboard the ship? A possibility, although he might be relying entirely on the hidden tanks of anaesthetic gas.

Second, were either or both of the other men his accomplices? Again a possibility, but distinctly less strong.

124

Third, and a less simple set of circumstances: What would happen when the ship reached Dasce's dead star? Here again variables piled on variables. Did Malagate know of Dasce's hideaway? If so, would he recognize it on sight? The answers here were both *Probably yes.*

The question then would be, how to surprise and either capture or kill Hildemar Dasce without hindrance from Malagate.

Gersen reached a decision. Detteras had urged the need for amicability. One thing was sure: amicability would be sternly tested before long.

Time passed; a wary routine was established. Gersen chose a propitious time and gave the body of Suthiro to space. The ship slid effortlessly past shining stars, at astounding speed, by means only vaguely comprehensible to the men who controlled it.

The pale of human civilization and law came to an end; at some precise instant the ship passed Beyond and struck up and out toward the dwindling fringes of the galaxy. Gersen kept steady if discreet surveillance over his three shipmates, wondering who would first show concern, anxiety, or suspicion as to the immediate destination.

This person was Kelle, though any of the three might have been muttering together out of Gersen's hearing. "Where the devil are we headed?" Kelle inquired peevishly. "This is no area to attract a locater; we're practically in intergalactic space."

Gersen took up a relaxed position. "I have not been altogether candid with you three gentlemen."

Three faces turned swiftly, three pairs of eyes bored in at him.

"What do you mean?" grated Detteras.

"It is not a serious matter. I have been compelled to make a detour. After I perform a certain errand, we will proceed with our original plans." He raised his hand as Detteras took a deep breath. "It serves no purpose to admonish me; the situation is unavoidable."

Warweave spoke in an icy voice: "What is this 'situation'?"

"I'll be glad to explain, and I'm sure all of you will appreciate my predicament. First of all, I seem to have made an enemy of a well-known criminal. He is known as Malagate the Woe." Gersen glanced from face to face. "Doubtless you all have heard of him; he is one of the Demon Princes. The day before we left one of his lieutenants, a creature named Hildemar Dasce, kidnaped a young woman I happen

125

to be interested in and conveyed her to a private world. I feel obligated to this young woman; she is suffering through no fault of her own, but merely from Malagate's desire to punish or intimidate me. I believe I have located Dasce's planet; I plan to rescue this young woman, and I hope for your cooperation."

Detteras spoke in a voice thick with rage. "Why could you not have told us of your plans before we left? You insisted on leaving, you forced us to break our engagments at great inconvenience—"

Gersen said mildly, "You have some cause for resentment, but, since my own time is limited, I thought it best to combine the two projects." He grinned as Detteras' neck swelled in new fury. "With luck, this business will not take long, and we will be on our way without delay."

Kelle said meditatively, "The kidnaper has conveyed the young woman to a world in this vicinity?"

"I think so. I hope so."

"And you expect our help in rescuing this young woman?"

"Only in a passive sense. I merely ask that you don't interfere with my plans."

"Suppose that the kidnaper resents your intrusion. Suppose that he kills you."

"The possibility exists. But I have the advantage of surprise. He must feel completely secure, and probably I will have no great trouble overpowering him."

"Overpowering him?" inquired Warweave, delicately sardonic.

"Overpowering or killing him."

At this moment the Jarnell kicked out, the ship whined down into ordinary velocities. Ahead glowed a dim red star. If it were double, its companion was yet invisible.

Gersen said, "As I say, surprise is my most important asset, so therefore I must ask that none of you through inadvertence or malice use the radio." Gersen already had disabled the radio, but he saw no reason to put Malagate on his guard. "I'll explain my plans so that there can be no misunderstanding. First, I'll bring the ship close enough to inspect the surface of the planet, but far enough out to avoid radar detection. If my theories are correct and I locate Dasce's habitation, I'll go to the far side of the world, approach the surface, and land as close to Dasce's dwelling as feasible. Then I'll take the platform flyer and do what must be done. The three of you need only wait till I return; then we shall be once more on our way to Teehalt's planet. I know I can count on your cooperation, because I naturally shall take the monitor filament with me and hide it somewhere before I confront Hildemar Dasce. If I am killed, the filament will be lost. Naturally I will need the weapons which are now in the security locker, but I see no reason for objection on your part."

No one spoke. Gersen, looking from one to another, studying most intently the face of his suspect, laughed inwardly. Malagate was posed with a maddening dilemma. If he should interfere and by some means warn Dasce, then Gersen might well be killed and Malagate's hopes of acquiring Tee-halt's planet dashed. Would he trade Dasce for the planet? Gersen was certain of his decision; Malagate was notoriously callous.

Detteras heaved a deep sigh. "Gersen, you're a subtle man. You've put us in a position where, for motives of sweet reason, we are forced to do your bidding."

"I assure you that my motives are irreproachable."

"Yes, yes, the damsel in distress. All very well; we ourselves would be criminals to deny her the chance of rescue. My exasperation is not at your goals—if you have told us the truth—but at your lack of candor."

With nothing to lose, Gersen became humble. "Yes, perhaps I should have explained more carefully. But I am accustomed to working by myself. In any event, the situation is now as I have described it. Do I have the cooperation of you all?"

"Humph," said Warweave. "We have little choice, as you are perfectly well aware."

"Mr. Kelle?" asked Gersen.

Kelle inclined his head.

"Mr. Detteras?"

"As Warweave points out, we have no choice."

"In that case I will proceed with my plans. The world on which we are to land, incidentally, is a dead star rather than a planet."

"Does not excessive gravity make habitation inconvenient?" asked Kelle.

"We'll know very shortly."

Warweave turned away, went to look out at the red dwarf. The dark companion had now become visible: a large brown-gray disk, three times the diameter of Alphanor, mottled and reticulated in black and umber. Gersen was pleased to find surrounding space rich in detritus; the radar screen indicated dozens of minuscule planetoids and moonlets in orbits about each star. He could approach the dead star boldly with small fear of detection. A momentary shift into inter-split braked the ship; another brought it to a state of lazy drifting a quarter-million miles above the now looming mass.

The surface seemed dim and featureless, with vast areas covered by what looked like oceans of chocolate-colored dust. The outline of the world was sharp and stark against the black of space, indicating a sparse atmosphere. Gersen went to the macroscope, inspected the surface. The world's relief leapt into perspective, though the terrain still was hardly rugged. Chains of volcanic mountains netted the surface; there was a mesh of rifts and crevasses, a number of ancient isolated plutonic buttes, hundreds of volcanos, some active, others dead or quiescent.

Gersen set crossbars on a short sharp peak at the demarcation between day and night; the object seemed not to move, nor to alter its position in relation to the line of darkness: apparently the world held a constant face to its companion. In such case, Dasce's dwelling would almost certainly be on the bright face, probably near the equator, at the longitude directly under the sun. He scrutinized the region carefully, under high magnification. The area was large; there were dozens of volcanic craters, large and small.

Gersen searched for an hour. Warweave, Kelle and Detteras stood watching him with varying degrees of impatience and sardonic dislike.

Gersen reviewed his logic; it seemed to hang together. The red dwarf had been listed on a well-used page in Dasce's *Directory;* it was found within the requisite ellipsoidal shell; it had a dark star companion. This *must* be the star. And, by every likelihood, Dasce's crater must be located somewhere within the warm sunlit area below.

An odd formation attracted his attention: a square plateau, with five mountain ranges radiating like the fingers of a hand. A phrase of the Melnoy Heights Imp occurred to him: "Thumbnail Gulch." At fullest magnification Gersen examined the area corresponding to the thumbnail. Certainly there was a small crater here. Certainly it seemed to show a slightly different color, a slightly different texture than the others. And there where the sunlight struck glancingly on the inside wall, a glint? And below, the faint shine of white?

Gersen reduced the magnification, studied the surrounding terrain. Even though Dasce might not detect approaching ships at planetary distances, his radar might warn him of

128

ships approaching for a landing. If he dropped down on the far side of the world and then slanted in behind the horizon, to land behind the plateau which formed the palm of the hand, he might well be able to surprise Dasce.

He fed the necessary information into the course computer, engaged the autopilot. The ship veered and began its descent.

Kelle, unable to contain his curiosity, asked, "Well? Have you found what you were looking for?"

"I think so," said Gersen. "I can't be certain."

"If you are careless enough to be killed," said Kelle, "you put us to enormous inconvenience."

Gersen nodded. "This is essentially what I meant to convey to you a short while ago. I am sure that you'll help me, at least passively."

"We have already agreed to this."

The dark star loomed below and the ship landed on a shelf of naked brown stone a quarter mile from a heave of low black hills. The stone was the texture of brick; the surrounding plain displayed a surface resembling dried brown mud.

Overhead the red dwarf bulked large; the ship cast a dense black shadow. A thin wind blew small curls of dust across the plain, sifting a greenish-blue powder into long herringbone drifts.

Detteras said thoughtfully, "You know, I think it only fair that you leave the filament here. Why victimize us?"

"I don't plan to be killed, Mr. Detteras."

"You're plans might go awry."

"If so, your troubles will seem very trivial in comparison to mine. May I have my weapons?"

The locker was opened; the three watched warily while Gersen armed himself. He looked from face to face. In the mind of one of these men feverish plots were hatching. Would he act as Gersen anticipated—which was to say, not act? Here was a chance Gersen must take. Suppose he were wrong, suppose this were not Dasce's planet and Malagate knew it; suppose Malagate, through some intuition, suspected Gersen's goal. He might be ready to sacrifice his hopes of acquiring Teehalt's world in order to maroon Gersen out here on this dark star. There was a precaution Gersen could take; it would be foolish for him not to do so. He stepped back into the engine room and detached a small but vital component from the energy reactor, one which could be refabricated, if necessary, with ingenuity and patience. He tucked it into his pouch, along with the filament. Warweave,

129

standing in the doorway, observed the act but made no comment.

Gersen dressed himself in an airsuit, left the ship. Opening the forward hatch, he winched down the little platform flyer, loaded aboard a spare airsuit and spare tanks of oxygen, and without further ceremony set out for Thumbnail Gulch, skimming low to the ground, the thin atmosphere keening over the windshield.

The landscape was odd even to one accustomed to the terrain of strange planets: a dark spongy surface in varying shades of maroon, brown and gray, marred here and there by volcanic cones and low wallowing black hills. This might be true star stuff—clinker remaining after the fires had died —or it might be sediment swept up from space. Most likely both. Gersen wondered, did the awareness that he was traversing the surface of a dead star contribute to the sense of weirdness and unreality? The thin atmosphere allowed absolute clarity of vision; the horizons were far, the panorama seemed endless. And overhead there was the glowering sphere of the red dwarf, filling an eighth of the sky.

The ground shouldered up to become the plateau which comprised the palm of the hand; a titanic flow of lava. Gersen swerved to the right. Far ahead he could see a line of black hills laying across the landscape like the back of a monstrous petrified triceratops. This was the "thumb" at the end of which rose Dasce's volcano. Gersen flew low to the ground, taking advantage of all possible cover, swerving in and out, close to the wall of the plateau, and so approached the line of jagged black peaks.

Slowly, cautiously, he eased up the tumbled slope, jets muffled by the thin air to no more than a mutter. Dasce might have installed detectors along these slopes—but, on second thought, it seemed hardly likely. He would consider the effort superfluous. Why attack by land when a torpedo from space would be easier?

Gersen gained the ridge. There, two miles ahead, was the volcano which he hoped would be Dasce's hideaway. Off to the side, down on the plain which continued on and on indefinitely, was the most welcome sight of Gersen's experience, a sight which brought tears of sheer savage heart-rending joy to his eyes: a small spaceboat. His hypothesis had been correct: here was Thumbnail Gulch in all certainty; here would be found Hildemar Dasce. And Pallis Atwrode?

Gersen landed the platform and continued on foot, taking advantage of all possible cover, avoiding approaches where

130

detectors would be most likely, even though caution seemed no more than a formality. Destiny could not bring him this far only to deal him failure! He mounted the slopes: mingled basalt, obsidian and tuff. Reaching the lip of the crater, he peered over—out on a webbed dome constructed of thin cables and transparent film, held distended by air pressure. The crater was not large: fifty yards in diameter and almost perfectly cylindrical, the walls being formed of striated volcanic glass.

At the bottom of the crater Dasce had made a careless attempt at landscaping. There were a pond of brackish water, a clump of palm trees, a tangle of rank vines. Gersen looked an implacable god, a god of vengeance.

In the center of the crater was a cage, and in the cage sat a naked man: tall, haggard, his face a ghastly wreck, his body crooked, marked with a hundred welts. Gersen remembered Suthiro's explanation of how Dasce lost his eyelids. Looking again, he remembered the photographs in Dasce's parlor: this man was the subject of the photographs.

Gersen looked elsewhere. Directly below was a pavilion of black cloth, a series of connected tents. There was no sign of Hildemar Dasce. Entrance to the crater was apparently by way of a tunnel leading through the wall of the volcano.

Gersen moved carefully around the lip, looked down over the slope. The porous brown-black plain extended limitlessly off in three directions. Nearby rested the spaceboat, seeming no larger than a toy in the clarity of the atmosphere, on the endlessness of the plain.

Gersen turned his attention back to the dome. With a knife he cut a small slit in the film, then settled himself to watch.

Ten minutes passed before the pressure drop activated a warning signal. Out from one of the tents charged Hildemar Dasce. Gersen saw him with savage delight. He wore loose white pantaloons and no more. His torso, stained a faded purple, was ribbed with muscle. He stared up with lidless eyes, the blue cheeks blooming from the vermilion face.

Dasce marched across the crater floor. The prisoner within the cage followed him attentively with his gaze.

Dasce vanished from sight. Gersen hid in a crevice. Dasce presently emerged on the plain in an airsuit, carrying a case. He mounted the crater wall with strong easy strides, passing close by Gersen.

Dasce put down the case, brought forth a projector, swept a beam of radiation over the surface of the dome. The escaping air, evidently dosed with a fluorescent agent, glowed yellow. Dasce went to the cut and bent over it, and Gersen felt his instant suspicion. He straightened up and looked all around. Gersen crouched back out of sight.

When he looked once more, Dasce was at work mending the rip with cement and a new strip of film. The entire operation required but a minute. Then Dasce replaced the unused material and the projector into the case, straightened up. He made another careful scrutiny of rim, slope and plain; then, suspicion blunted, he started back down the slope.

Gersen rose from his hiding place and followed, not fifty feet behind.

Dasce, jumping from rock to rock down the slope, failed to look back—until Gersen dislodged a rock which bounded ahead and past. Dasce stopped, turned sharply. Gersen was out of sight behind a jut of rock, grinning in a kind of mad glee.

Dasce proceeded. Gersen followed close behind. At the base of the slope a sound, a vibration, alarmed Dasce. Once more he turned to look up-slope—directly at the figure leaping down on him. Gersen laughed to see the loose pale mouth open in startlement, and then he struck. Dasce toppled, rolled, bounded to his feet, started to run awkwardly for the airlock; Gersen fired at the back of one of the rangy thighs. Dasce fell.

Gersen seized him by the ankles, dragged him into the airlock, slammed the outer door. Dasce struggled and kicked, the red and blue face hideously contorted. Gersen pointed the projac, but Dasce merely tried to kick it from his grasp. Gersen fired again, numbing Dasce's other leg. Dasce lay still, glaring like a boar at bay. With a roll of tape brought hopefully for such a purpose, Gersen lashed Dasce's ankles. Then warily he seized the right arm, bent it back and around. Dasce was forced over on his face. Presently, after a struggle, his arms were taped behind his back. The lock mechanism automatically had filled the space with air; Gersen now removed the vitrine globe from Dasce's head.

"We renew our acquaintance," said Gersen in a voice of hushed, reverent joy.

Dasce said nothing.

Gersen dragged him out into the floor of the crater. The prisoner jumped to his feet, pressed himself to the bars of the cage, stared at Gersen as if he were an archangel with wings, trumpet and aureole.

132

Gersen assured himself as to the security of Dasce's bonds, ran over to the tent, projac ready for an unexpected servitor or comrade-in-arms of Dasce's. The prisoner looked after him with astounded, unbelieving eyes.

Pallis Atwrode lay huddled under a limp dirty sheet, face to the wall. There was no one else. Gersen touched her on the shoulder, and fascinatedly watched her flesh crawl. His exultation became mingled with horror, to produce a queer stomach-twisting emotion such as he had never before even imagined. "Pallis," he said, "Pallis—it's Kirth Gersen." The words reached her, muffled by the globe which Gersen still wore; she only crouched and huddled more tightly. Gerson rolled her over; she lay with her eyes shut. Her face, once so gay and impudent and charming, was bleak and austere. "Pallis," called Gersen, "open your eyes. It's Kirth Gersen! You're safe!"

She shook her head slightly, held her eyes tight shut.

Gersen turned away. At the door to the tent he looked back. Her eyes were wide open, staring in wonder, but she instantly closed them again.

Gersen left her, investigated the entire crater, reassured himself that no one else was present, and returned to Dasce.

"Nice place you've got here, Dasce," said Gersen in a conversational tone. "A little hard to find when your friends want to drop in."

"How did you find me?" said Dasce in a guttural voice. "No one knows of this place."

"Except your boss."

"He doesn't know."

"How do you think I found out?"

Dasce was silent. Gersen went to the cage, unbarred the door, motioned to the prisoner, wondering whether the man's mind had also failed him. "Come out."

The prisoner limped haltingly forward. "Who are you?"

"No matter. You are free."

"Free?" The man worked his loose jaws over the word, turned to look toward Dasce. He spoke in a reverent voice. "What of—him?"

"I shall kill him presently."

The man said softly, "This must be a dream."

Gersen returned to Pallis. She was sitting on the bed, the sheet clutched around her. Her eyes were open. She looked at Gersen, rose to her feet, fainted. Gersen lifted her, carried her out to the crater floor. The erstwhile captive stood looking at Dasce from a respectful distance. Gersen spoke to him. "What is your name?"

The man looked momentarily bewildered. He knit his brows as if trying to remember. "I am Robin Rampold," he said at last in a soft hushed voice. "And you—you are *his* enemy?"

"I am his executioner. His nemesis."

"It is a marvel!" breathed Rampold. "After so long that I cannot remember the beginning...." Tears began to course down his cheeks. He looked at the cage, walked over to it, studied it, then looked back at Gersen. "I know this place well. Each crack, each crevice, each fleck and crystal of the metal." His voice faded. Suddenly he asked, "What is the year?"

"1524."

Rampold seemed to become smaller. "I did not know it was so long; I have forgotten so much." He looked up toward the dome. "There is no day or night here—nothing but the red sun. When *he* is gone, there are no events.... Seventeen years I have stood in that cage. And now I am out." He walked over to Dasce, stood looking down at him. Gersen followed. Rampold said, "Long, long ago we were two different people. I taught him a lesson. I made him suffer. The memory is all that has kept me alive."

Dasce laughed a harsh cackle. "I have sought to repay you." He glanced up toward Gersen. "Best kill me while you can, or I will do the same to you."

Gersen stood reflecting. Dasce must die. There would be no compunction when the time came. But behind the red forehead was knowledge which Gersen needed. How to extract this knowledge? Torture? Gersen suspected that Dasce would laugh while being torn limb from limb. Trickery? Subtlety? He looked speculatively down into the coarse red and blue face. Dasce did not flinch.

Gersen turned to Rampold. "Can you navigate Dasce's spaceboat?"

Rampold sadly shook his head.

"Then I suppose you must come with me."

Rampold spoke in a tremulous voice. "What of—*him?*"

"Eventually I'll kill him."

Rampold said in a low voice, "Give him to me."

"No." Gersen returned to the inspection of Dasce. Somehow he must be made to reveal the identity of Malagate. A direct question would be worse than useless. "Dasce," he asked, "why did you bring Pallis Atwrode out here?"

134

"She was too beautiful to kill," said Dasce easily.

"And why should you kill her?"

"I enjoy killing beautiful women."

Gersen grinned. Dasce possibly hoped to provoke him. "You may or may not live to regret your sins."

"Who sent you here?" asked Dasce.

"Someone who knew."

Dasce slowly shook his head. "There is only one, and he never sent you."

So much for that ploy, thought Gersen. Dasce would not easily be deceived. Well then. He would take Dasce aboard the ship. The situation was certain to produce some sort of reaction.

Now a new problem. He did not dare leave Robin Rampold alone with Dasce, not even for long enough too fetch the platform. Rampold might kill Dasce. Or Dasce might command Rampold to release him. After seventeen years of degradation, Rampold might be sufficiently under Dasce's influence to obey. And Pallis Atwrode—what of her?

He turned to find her standing in the doorway, the sheet clutched around her, watching him with a wide troubled gaze. He approached her and she shrank back. Gersen was uncertain whether or not she recognized him. "Pallis—it's Kirth Gersen."

She nodded somberly. "I know." She looked at the prone form of Hildemar Dasce. "You've tied him up," she said in a voice of troubled wonder.

"That's the least of his worries."

She looked at him warily. Gersen found himself unable to fathom her thoughts. "You're—you're not his friend?"

Gersen felt an entirely new type of sickness. "No. I'm not his friend. Of course not. Did he say so?"

"He said ... he said...." She turned to stare in perplexity at Dasce.

"Don't believe anything he told you." He looked into her face, wondering as to the extent of her confusion and shock. "Are you—all right?"

She refused to meet his eyes. Gersen said gently, "I'm taking you back to Avente. You're safe now." She nodded stonily. If she would only evince some emotion! Relief—tears—even reproaches!

Gersen sighed, turned away. The problem still remained: how to convey all of them to the platform. He dared leave neither Pallis nor Rampold alone with Dasce; he had enjoyed domination over them both too long.

135

Gersen replaced the vitrine globe over Dasce's head and dragged him through the tunnel, out upon the plain, where the two within could not see him.

* * * * * * *

Jets roaring at full power, the overloaded platform lurched sluggishly around the plateau, blowing up a fan of dust which settled with startling rapidity in the thin atmosphere. Ahead stood the spaceship, minute against the sweep of the vast horizon. Gersen landed close beside the entrance port. Hand weapon within easy reach, he climbed the accommodation ladder. Inside, Attel Malagate had watched his approach, had seen the cargo. Malagate could not know what Dasce had told Gersen. He must be taut with indecision. Dasce, who would recognize the ship, must suspect but could not be sure that Malagate was aboard.

The airlock thudded shut, the pumps throbbed, the inner door swung open. Gersen stepped forward. Kelle, Detteras, Warweave sat at various quarters of the room. They looked at him without friendliness. No one made a move.

Gersen unfastened the head globe. "I'm back."

"So we see," said Detteras.

"I've been successful," said Gersen. "I've got a captive with me: Hildemar Dasce. A word of warning to you. This man is a brutal murderer. He is desperate. I intend to hold him under rigid conditions. I ask that none of you interfere or have anything to do with this man. The other two persons are a man Dasce has kept penned in a cage for seventeen years, and a young woman whom Dasce recently kidnaped and whose mind may have suffered in consequence. She shall use my cabin. I shall keep Dasce in the cargo hold. The other man, Robin Rampold, will no doubt be happy for the use of a settee."

"This voyage becomes stranger by the hour," said Warweave.

Detteras rose impatiently to his feet. "Why do you bring this man Dasce aboard? I'm surprised you haven't killed him."

"Consider me squeamish, if you like."

Detteras gave a bark of sour laughter. "Let us proceed; we are anxious to get this trip over as fast as possible."

Gersen sent Rampold into the ship with Pallis Atwrode, then slid the platform under the winch, lifted the platform with Dasce aboard into the cargo hold, where he removed Dasce's head globe. Dasce glared at him wordlessly.

"You may see someone aboard you recognize," said Gersen. He doesn't want his identity made known to his two colleagues, as it would interfere with his plans. You will be wise to keep a still tongue in your head."

Dasce said nothing. Gersen secured him with exceeding care. At the center of a long cable he made a loop which he knotted and clamped tightly around Dasce's neck. The ends of the cable he made fast at opposite sides of the hold, stretching the cable taut. Dasce was now constricted in the middle of the hold, the cable extending past him to right and left, the ends ten feet out of his reach to either side. Even with hands free Dasce could not work himself loose. Gersen now cut the tapes binding Dasce's arms and legs. Dasce instantly struck out. Gersen dodged aside, clubbed Dasce with the butt of his weapon. Dasce reeled over senseless. Gersen slipped off Pasce's airsuit, searched the pockets of the white pantaloons, found nothing. He made a final check of the bonds, then returned to the main saloon, bolting the hatch behind him.

Rampold had divested himself of his airsuit and sat quietly in a corner. Detteras and Kelle had done the same for Pallis Atwrode, and had helped her into spare clothing. She sat now to the side of the cabin drinking coffee, her face wan and pinched, her eyes dark and musing. Kelle cast a glance of disapprobation toward Gersen. "This is Miss Atwrode—the receptionist at the department. What in the name of heaven is your connection with her?"

"The answer is perfectly simple," said Gersen. "I met her the first day I visited the university, and asked her out for the evening. For reasons of sheer spite or malice, or so I suppose, Hildemar Dasce struck me down and kidnaped her. I felt it was my duty to rescue her, and I've done so."

Kelle smiled thinly. "I suppose we can't fault you for this."

Warweave spoke in the driest of voices: "Presumably we will now make for our original destination."

"That is certainly my intention."

"I suggest then that we proceed."

"Yes," grumbled Detteras. "The sooner we put a term to this fantastic voyage the better."

* * * * * * *

The dark star and its feeble red companion became one with space. In the hold Hildemar Dasce, recovering consciousness, swore in a low vile mutter, testing his bonds with insensate ferocity. He tore and twisted at the clamps till the skin peeled from his fingers; he plucked at the metal strands in the cable till his fingernails broke. Then he tried a new procedure. Thrusting against the floor, lunging from side to side, he tried to pull the cable loose from where it was fastened at the walls: first to the right, then to the left. He succeeded only in bruising his neck. Assured that he was in fact helpless, though hands and feet were free, he relaxed, panting. His mind seethed with emotion. How had Gersen located the dark star? No one alive knew the location but himself. And Malagate. Dasce reviewed the occasions on which he had circumvented, cheated, or failed Malagate, and wondered if one of these occasions might not have come home to roost.

In the saloon, Gersen sat brooding on a settee. The three men from the university—one of whom was not a man— stood together far forward. There was Kelle: suave, fastidious, compact in physique; Warweave: ectomorphic, saturnine; Detteras: large-bodied, restless, moody. Gersen eyed his suspect, probing his every act, word, and gesture for corroboration, for some sign to provide the absolute assurance he needed. Pallis Atwrode sat quietly nearby, lost in reverie. From time to time her face twitched, her fingers clenched into her palms. There would be no qualms about the killing of Hildemar Dasce. Robin Rampold stood listlessly at the microfilm library, looking at the index, stroking his long bony chin.

He turned, glanced toward Gersen, sidled across the room wolfishly. In a voice so polite as to seem servile he asked, "*He*—is *he* alive?"

"For the moment."

Rampold hesitated, opened his mouth, closed it again. Finally he asked diffidently, "What do you plan for him?"

"I don't know," said Gersen. "I want to make use of him."

Rampold became very earnest. He spoke in a low voice, as if afraid that the other occupants of the saloon would hear. "Why not put him into my charge? Then you would be relieved of the effort of guarding and tending him."

"No," said Gersen, "I think not."

138

Rampold's face became even more haggard and desperate. "But—I must."

"You must?"

Rampold nodded. "You cannot understand. For seventeen years he has been—" he could not find words. Finally he said, "He has been the center of my existence. He has been like a personal god. He has provided food and drink and pain. Once he brought me a kitten—a beautiful black kitten. He watched as I touched it, smiling as if benign. This time I thwarted him. I killed the little creature, at once. Because I knew his plan. He wanted to wait until I came to love it, then *he* would kill it—torture it where I could watch.... Of course he made me pay."

Gersen drew a deep breath. "He has too much power over you. I can't trust you with him."

Tears began to form in Rampold's eyes. He spoke in a series of disjointed sentences. "It is strange. I feel grief now. What I feel for him I cannot put into words. It goes to an extreme and beyond and becomes almost tenderness. Substances can be so sweet that they taste bitter, so sour that they taste salt.... Yes, I would care for him with great pains. I would devote the rest of my life to him." He held out his hands. "Give him to me. I have nothing, or I would repay you."

Gersen could only shake his head. "We will talk of this later."

Rampold nodded heavily, returned across the room. Gersen looked forward to where Detteras, Kelle and Warweave continued a desultory conversation. Apparently they were agreed, tacitly or otherwise, on a policy of disinterest toward the new passengers. Gersen smiled grimly. He who was Malagate would not care to confront Hildemar Dasce. Dasce's temperament was not a subtle one; he was as likely as not to blurt out some damaging disclosure. Malagate would certainly try for a few quiet words of warning and reassurance, or conceivably an opportunity to murder Dasce discreetly.

The situation was unstable; sooner or later it was bound to collapse into more truthful relationships. Gersen toyed with the idea of precipitating the climax, perhaps by bringing Dasce into the saloon or taking Kelle, Detteras and Warweave into the cargo hold.... He decided to bide his time. He still carried his weapons; the three from the university, apparently assured of his good intentions, had not required that he restore them to the locker. Amazing, thought Gersen:

139

even now Malagate could have no cause to suspect that Gersen stalked him. He would be less wary than he might be, and, using the pretext of curiosity, might well seek to look in on Dasce.

Vigilance, thought Gersen. It occurred to him that Robin Rampold would be a useful ally in this situation. No matter what distortions and sublimations seventeen years had produced, he would be no less alert than Gersen himself in any matter relating to Hildemar Dasce.

Gersen rose to his feet and went aft, through the engine room, into the cargo hold. Dasce, making no pretense of stoic resignation, glared at him. Gersen noted Dasce's bleeding fingers and, putting his projac on a shelf to void the possibility of Dasce's wresting it away from him, stepped close to check Dasce's bonds. Dasce kicked savagely. Gersen hacked him behind the ear with the side of his hand, and Dasce fell back. Gersen assured himself as to the clamps which constricted the cable around Dasce's neck, then moved back, out of his reach.

"It seems," said Gersen, "that troubles are catching up with you."

Dasce spat at him. Gersen jumped back. "You're in a poor case for such offensiveness."

"Fah! What more can you do to me? Do you think I fear death? I live only out of hate."

"Rampold has asked that I give you into his care."

Dasce sneered. "He fears me until he reeks and crawls. He is soft as honey. It was no longer gratifying to hurt him."

"I wonder how long it will take to make the same sort of man out of you."

Dasce spat once more. Then he said, "Tell me how you found my star."

"I had information."

"From whom?"

"What difference does it make?" said Gersen. He thought to insert an idea into Dasce's mind. "You'll never have the opportunity of paying him off."

Dasce pulled back his mouth in a hideous grin. "Who is aboard this ship?"

Gersen made no reply. Standing back in the shadows, he watched Dasce. He must suspect, to the point of certainty, that Malagate was aboard. Dasce could be no less uncertain than Malagate himself.

Gersen framed and discarded a half-dozen questions calculated to trick Malagate's name from Dasce. The best were either too clumsy or too subtle; the worst would apprise Dasce that Gersen wanted information, and so put him on his guard.

Dasce tried to wheedle. "Come! As you say, I am helpless, at your mercy. I am interested in learning who betrayed me."

"Who do you think it might be?"

Dasce grinned ingenuously. "I have a number of enemies. For instance, the Sarkoy. Was it he?"

"The Sarkoy is dead."

"Dead!"

"He helped you kidnap the young woman. I poisoned him."

"Fah," spat Dasce. "Women are everywhere. Why become excited? Release me. I have wealth and I will pay you half if you tell me who betrayed me."

"It was not Suthiro the Sarkoy."

"Tristano? Surely not Tristano. How could he know?"

"When I met Tristano he had little to say."

"Who then?"

Gersen said, "Very well, I'll tell you; why not? One of the administrators at the Sea Province University gave me the information."

Dasce rubbed his hand over his mouth, looked sidewise at Gersen in suspicion and doubt. "Why should he do so?" he muttered. "I can't understand any of this."

Gersen had hoped to surprise an exclamation from Dasce. He asked, "Do you know to whom I refer?"

But Dasce only looked at him blankly. Gersen picked up his projac, left the hold.

Returning to the saloon, he found conditions as before. He signaled Robin Rampold back into the engine room. "You asked that Dasce might be put into your charge."

Rampold eyed him in tremulous excitement. "Yes!"

"I cannot do this—but I need your help in guarding him."

"Of course!"

"Dasce is tricky. You must never enter the cargo hold." Rampold winced in disappointment.

"Equally important, you must not allow anyone else near the cargo hold. These men are Dasce's enemies. They might kill him."

"No, no!" exclaimed Rampold. "Dasce must not die!"

Gersen had a new thought. Malagate had ordained the death of Pallis Atwrode for fear that unwittingly she might reveal his identity. In her present state she posed no

141

threat; nevertheless, she might recover. Malagate might well wish to destroy her, if he could do so without risk. Gersen said, "Also, you must try to guard Pallis Atwrode, and make sure that no one disturbs her."

Rampold was less interested. "I will do what you ask."

Chapter 11

From "The Avatar's Apprentice," in *Scroll from the Ninth Dimension:*

Intelligence? asked Marmaduke at one of the permitted intervals, as he attended the EMINENCE upon the Parapet. What is intelligence?

Why, responded the EMINENCE, it is no more than a human occupation; an activity which men put their brains to, as a frog kicks his legs to swim; it is a standard which men in their egotism use to measure other and perhaps nobler races, who are thereby dumfounded.

Do you mean, REVEREND GRAY, that no living creature other than man can share the quality of intelligence?

But ha! And why should I not ask, what is LIFE, what is LIVING, but a disease of the primordial slime, a purulence in the original candid mud, which culminates through cycles and degrees, by distillations and sediments, in the human manifestation?

But, REVEREND, it is known that other worlds demonstrate this fact of LIFE. I allude to the jewels of Olam, as well as the folk of the Chthonian Bog.

Witling, how have you glanced off the exact stroke of the ESSENCE.

REVEREND, I crave your indulgence.

The way along the Parapet is not to the forward-footed.

REVEREND GRAY, I pray that my direction be defined.

Eight tones of the gong have sounded. Be content for the nonce, and fetch the morning wine.

* * * * * * *

The filament from Lugo Teehalt's monitor fed impulses into

the computer, which digested the information, combined it
with the equations describing the ship's previous position, and
despatched instructions to the autopilot which swerved the
ship off and away, on a course roughly parallel to the line
between Alphanor and Smade's Planet. Time passed. Life
within the ship fell into a routine. Gersen, assisted by Robin
Rampold, guarded the cargo hold, though Gersen forbade
Rampold entry into the hold itself. For the first few days
Hildemar Dasce evinced a brassy jocularity, alternating with
earnest threats of vengeance at the hands of an agent he
refused to identify.

"Ask Rampold what he thinks," said Dasce, leering from his
bright blue lidless eyes. "Do you want this happening to
you?"

"No," said Gersen. "I don't think it's going to happen."

Occasionally Dasce demanded that Gersen answer his
questions. "Where are you taking me?" he would ask. "Back
to Alphanor?"

"No."

"Where, then?"

"You'll see."

"Answer me, or by—" here Dasce swore obscene oaths
"—I'll do you worse than you've ever imagined!"

"It's a chance we have to take," said Gersen.

"We?" asked Dasce softly. "Who is 'we'?"

"Don't you know?"

"Why doesn't he come in here? Tell him I want to talk
to him."

"Any time he wants he can come in."

At which Dasce fell silent. Goad, prod, pry as he might,
Gersen never could induce Dasce to utter a name. Nor did
any of the three from the university show interest in Dasce.
As for Pallis Atwrode, her detachment at first was profound.
For hours she sat, looking out at the passing stars. She ate,
slowly, hesitantly, without hunger; she slept for hours on
end, curled into as tight a ball as possible. Then gradually
she returned to the present, and at times became something
like the carefree Pallis Atwrode of old.

The overcrowded confines of the ship made it impossible
for Gersen to talk to her in private, which, in his estima-
tion, was as well. The situation, with Dasce in the hold and
Attel Malagate in the forward cabin, was already strained to
an almost unbearable degree of tautness.

More time passed. The ship traversed new regions, and regions after regions where no man had passed but one: Lugo

143

Teehalt. To all sides hung stars by the thousand, by the million: streaming, swarming, flowing, glaring, glittering; shifting silently one across the other, and the other across another still—worlds of infinite variety, populated by who knows whom; each drawing the eye, fixing the imagination, evoking wonder; each world an urge, a temptation, a mystery; each a promise of unseen sights, unknown knowledge, unsensed beauty.

Eventually a warm golden-white star showed dead ahead. The monitor panel blinked alternately green, red, green, red. The autopilot choked down the energy output; the split began to collapse; the ship set up a weird subsound as eddies and disturbances and backdrafts of a substance which could only be called space sucked at the ship's fabric.

The split collapsed with a slight shock; the ship slid serenely, like a boat drifting on a pond. The golden-white sun hung close at hand, controlling three planets. One was orange, small and near, a fuming cinder. Another swung in a far orbit, a gloomy dismal world, the color of tears. The third, sparkling green and blue and white, revolved close below the ship.

Gersen, Warweave, Detteras and Kelle, antagonisms temporarily set aside, bent over, the macroscope. The world was clearly beautiful, with a thick moist atmosphere, ample oceans, a varied topography.

Gersen was the first to stand away from the screen. The time had come to hone his vigilance to its sharpest edge. Warweave stood back next. "I'm completely satisfied. The planet is nonpareil. Mr. Gersen has not deceived us."

Kelle looked at him in surprise. "You think it unnecessary to land?"

"I think it unnecessary. But I am willing to land." He moved across the cabin, stood near the shelf to which was affixed Suthiro's switch. Gersen tensed. Is it to be Warweave? But Warweave passed on. Gersen released his pent breath. Of course the time was not yet. To profit from the gas, Malagate must somehow protect himself from its influence.

Kelle said, "I certainly believe that we should land, at least to make biometrics. In spite of its appearance the world may be completely unfriendly."

Detteras said doubtfully, "It's rather awkward, with captives and invalids and passengers. The sooner back to Alphanor the better."

Kelle snapped in a voice as sharp as any Gersen had heard him use. "You talk like a jackass. All this way,

144

merely to turn tail and run home? Obviously we must land, if only to walk out on the planet for five minutes!"

"Yes," said Detteras glumly. "No doubt you're right."

"Very well," said Warweave. "Down we go."

Gersen wordlessly swung the autopilot toggle over into the landing program. The horizons extended, the landscape became distinct: green parkland, low rolling hills, a chain of lakes to the north, a range of snow-clad crags to the south. The ship settled to the ground; the roar of exhaled energy ceased. There was now solidity underfoot, utter quiet except for the ticking of the automatic environment analyzer, which presently flashed three green lights: the optimum verdict.

There was a short wait for pressure equalization. Gersen and the three men from the university donned exterior clothing, rubbed allergen inhibitor on face, hands and neck, adjusted inhalators against bacteria and spores.

Pallis Atwrode looked from the observation ports in innocent wonder; Robin Rampold sidled uneasily along the back bulkhead like a lean old gray rat, making tentative motions, as if he wished to alight but did not dare leave the security of the saloon.

Air from outside flooded the boat, smelling fresh, damp, clean. Gersen went to the port, swung it open, made a polite if ironic gesture. "Gentlemen—your planet."

Warweave was the first to step down to the ground, with Detteras close behind, then Kelle. Gersen followed more slowly.

The monitor had brought them to a spot hardly a hundred yards from Lugo Teehalt's landing. Gersen thought the landscape even more entrancing than the photographs had suggested. The air was cool, scented with a vaguely herbaceous freshness. Across the valley, beyond a stand of tall dark trees, the hills rose, massive yet gentle, marked by outcrops of worn gray rock, the hollows holding copses of soft foliage. Beyond rose a single great billowing cloud castle, bright in the noon sunlight.

Across the meadow, on the far side of the river, Gersen saw what appeared to be a growth of flowering plants, and knew them to be the dryads. They stood at the edge of the forest, swaying on supple gray limbs, their movements easy and graceful. Magnificent creatures, thought Gersen, beyond a doubt—but somehow they were a—well, a discordant element. A perverse notion—but there it was. On their own planet they seemed out of place! Exotic elements in a scene as dear and beloved as—as what? Earth? Ger-

145

sen felt no conscious emotional attachment for Earth. Still, the world most nearly like this was Earth—or, more accurately, those occasional areas of Earth which somehow had evaded the artifices and modifications wrought by generations of man. This world was fresh, natural, unmodified. Except for the dryads—a jarring note—this might be Old Earth, Earth of the Golden Age, the Earth of natural man. . . .

Gersen felt a small exhilarating shock of enlightenment. Here resided the basic charm of the world: its near-identity to the environment in which man had evolved. Old Earth must have known many such smiling valleys; the feel of such landscapes permeated the entire fabric of the human psyche. Other worlds of the Oikumene might be pleasant and comfortable, but none were Old Earth; none of them were Home. . . . For a fact, mused Gersen, here is where I would like to build a cottage, with an old-fashioned garden, an orchard in the meadow, a rowboat tied to the riverbank. Dreams, idle yearning for the unattainable . . . but dreams and yearning which necessarily must affect every man. Gersen blinked at the impact of a new thought. Suddenly attentive, he watched the others.

Warweave stood by the riverbank frowning down into the water. Now he turned and shot a suspicious glance toward Gersen.

Kelle, beside a clump of ferns as high as his shoulder, looked first up to the head of the valley with its great white spire of cumulus, then down toward the far open parkland. The forest at either side of the valley formed an aisle, continuing till it melted and blurred into haze.

Detteras paced slowly along the meadow, hands behind his back. Now he bent, scooped up a handful of sod, worked it between his fingers, let the soil sift and fall. He turned to stare at the dryads. Kelle did the same.

The dryads, gliding slowly on supple legs, moved out of the shadows, toward the pool. Their fronds shone blue and magenta, copper-russet, gold-ocher. Intelligent beings?

Gersen turned once more to watch the three men. Kelle scowled faintly. Warweave inspected the dryads with obvious admiration. Detteras suddenly put his hands to his mouth and shrilled an ear-piercing whistle, to which the dryads seemed oblivious.

There was a sound from the ship; Gersen turned to see Pallis Atwrode descending the ladder. She raised her hands in the sunlight, drew a deep breath. "What a beautiful valley," she murmured. "Kirth, what a beautiful valley." She wandered slowly away, pausing now and then to look around her in delight.

Gersen, on sudden thought, turned and ran back up the ladder into the ship. Rampold—where was Rampold? Gersen hastened back to the cargo hold. Rampold had already entered. Gersen advanced cautiously, listened.

Dasce's voice came gruff, hoarse, full of a detestable exultation. "Rampold, do as I say. Do you hear me?"

"Yes, Hildemar."

"Go to the bulkhead, unloose the cable. Hurry now."

Gersen moved to where he could look unobserved into the hold. Rampold stood not four feet from Dasce, staring down into the red face.

"Do you hear me? Hurry, or I will cause you such grief you will bewail the day you were born."

Rampold laughed softly, quietly. "Hildemar, I have asked Kirth Gersen for you. I told him I would cherish you like a son, I would feed you the most nutritious foods, the most invigorating drink ... I do not think he will give you to me, so I must gulp down just a taste of the joy I have promised myself for seventeen years. I am now about to beat you to death. This is the first opportunity—"

Gersen stepped forward. "Sorry, Rampold, to interrupt."

Rampold uttered an inarticulate cry of utter desolation, turned, ran from the hold. Gersen followed him. In the engine room he made a careful adjustment of his projac, thrust it into a holster, returned to the cargo hold. Dasce bared his teeth like a wild animal.

"Rampold has no patience." He went to the bulkhead, began to unfasten the cable.

"What are you going to do?" Dasce demanded.

"The orders are that you shall be executed."

Dasce stared. "What orders?"

"You fool," said Gersen. "Can't you guess what's happened? I'm taking your old position." One side of the cable fell free. Gersen crossed the room. "Don't move unless you want me to break your leg." He unfastened the other end of the cable. "Now stand up. Walk slowly forward and down the ladder. Don't make a single wrong move or I'll shoot you."

Dasce rose slowly to his feet. Gersen motioned with his projac. "Move."

Dasce said, "Where are we?"

"Never mind where we are. Move."

Dasce slowly turned and, trailing the two long ends of

the cable, went foward—through the engine room, into the saloon, to the exit port. Here he hesitated, looked back over his shoulder. "Keep going," said Gersen.

Dasce descended the ladder. Gersen, following close, slipped on the trailing cable. He jumped to the ground and fell heavily, flat on his face. Dasce gave a wild raucous cry of exultation, leaped on him, seized the projac, sprang back.

Gersen slowly rose to his feet, backed away.

"Stop there," called Dasce. "Oho, but I have you now." He glanced around. Fifty feet to one side stood Warweave and Detteras, and slightly behind them Kelle. Pressed against the hull was Rampold. Dasce flourished the projac. "All of you, stand together while I decide what to do. Old Rampold, it's time he was dead. And Gersen, naturally, in the belly." He looked to where the three from the university stood. "And you—" he said to one of the men—"you played me false."

Gersen said, "You won't do yourself much good, Dasce."

"Oho, I won't? I hold the weapon. There's three here who are going to die. You, old Rampold, and Malagate."

"There's only a single charge in the gun. You may get one of us, but the others will get you."

Dasce turned a quick look at the charge indicator. He laughed harshly. "So be it. Who wants to die? Or rather, who do I want to kill?" He looked from face to face. "Old Rampold—I've had my pleasure from him. Gersen. Yes, I'd like to kill you. With a red-hot iron in your ear. And Malagate. You sly dog. You betrayed me. What your game is I don't know. Why you brought me here I don't know. But you're the one I'm going to kill." He raised the weapon, pointed, squeezed the trigger. Energy darted from the gun— but not the blazing blue bolt. Only a weak pale sizzle. It struck Warweave, knocked him to the ground. Gersen charged Dasce. Instead of fighting, Dasce hurled the weapon at Gersen's head, turned and ran up the valley. Gersen picked up the projac, snapped it open, inserted a fresh power pack.

He walked slowly forward to where Warweave was picking himself up from the ground. Detteras barked at Gersen, "You must be a moron, allowing such a man to take your gun."

Kelle spoke in a puzzled voice. "But why shoot Gyle Warweave? Is he a maniac?"

Gersen said, "I suggest we go back into the ship, where Mr. Warweave can rest. There was only a small charge in the gun, but no doubt it hurt."

148

Detteras grunted, turned toward the ship. Kelle took Warweave's arm, but Warweave shook him off and lurched up the accommodation ladder, followed by Detteras and Kelle, and finally Gersen.

Gersen asked Warweave, "Are you feeling better now?"

"Yes," said Warweave in a cold voice. "But I agree with Detteras. You displayed the utmost folly."

"I'm not so sure of that," said Gersen. "I carefully arranged the whole affair."

Detteras gaped at him stupidly. "Purposely?"

"I shorted out the projac, I arranged that Dasce could seize it, I informed him that there was a single charge left—so that he could verify my own conviction regarding the identity of Attel Malagate."

"Attel Malagate?" Kelle and Detteras stared blankly at Gersen. Warweave watched him narrow-eyed.

"Malagate the Woe. I've watched Mr. Warweave for a long time, feeling that he should more properly be known as Malagate."

"This is lunacy," gasped Detteras. "Are you serious?"

"Certainly I'm serious. It had to be either you, Warweave, or Kelle. I picked Warweave."

"Indeed," said Warweave. "May I ask why?"

"Of course. First of all I dismissed Detteras. He is an ugly man. Star Kings are more careful with their physiognomy."

"Star Kings?" blurted Detteras. "Who? Warweave? What nonsense!"

"Detteras likewise is a good eater, while Star Kings eat human food with disgust. As for Mr. Kelle, I also thought him an unlikely candidate. He is short and round—again not the physiognomy characteristic of a Star King."

Warweave's face twisted in a glacial smile. "You imply that a good appearance guarantees depravity of character?"

"No. I imply that Star Kings seldom leave their planet unless they can compete successfully against true men. Now, two other points. Kelle is married and has bred at least one daughter. Secondly, Kelle and Detteras have legitimate careers at the university. You are Honorary Provost and I remember something to the effect that a large endowment brought you the job."

"This is insanity," declared Detteras. "Warweave as Malagate the Woe. And a Star King to boot!"

"It's a fact," said Gersen.

"And what do you propose to do?"

"Kill him."

Detteras stared, then lunged forward, roaring in triumph as he grappled Gersen, only to grunt as Gersen twisted, swung an elbow, struck with the butt of the projac. Detteras reeled back.

"I want the cooperation of you and Mr. Kelle," said Gersen.

"Cooperate with a lunatic? Never!"

"Warweave is frequently absent from the university for long periods. Am I right? And one of these periods was only recently. Right?"

Detteras set his jaw. "I'll say nothing about that."

"This is true enough," said Kelle uneasily. He glanced sidewise at Warweave, then back to Gersen. "I assume you have strong reasons for your accusation."

"Certainly."

"I'd like to hear some of these reasons."

"They make a long story. It's enough to say that I tracked Malagate to the Sea Province University and narrowed the possibilities to you three. I suspected Warweave almost from the first, but I never was certain until the three of you stepped out on this planet."

"This is sheer farce," sighed Warweave wearily.

"This planet is like Earth—an Earth that no man alive has ever known; an Earth which hasn't existed for ten thousand years. Kelle and Detteras were entranced. Kelle drank in the view, Detteras reverently felt the soil. Warweave went to look into the water. Star Kings evolved from amphibious lizards who lived in wet holes. The dryads appeared. Warweave admired them, seemed to consider them ornamental. To Kelle and Detteras—and to myself—they are intruders. Detteras whistled at them, Kelle scowled. We men don't want fantastic creatures on a world so dear to us. But all this is theorizing. After I managed to capture Hildemar Dasce I went to great lengths to convince him that Malagate was his betrayer. When I gave him the chance he identified Warweave —with the projac."

Warweave shook his head pityingly. "I deny all your allegations." He looked to Kelle. "Do you believe me?"

Kelle pursed his lips. "Confound it, Gyle, I've come to regard Gersen as a competent man. I don't believe him to be either irresponsible or a lunatic."

Warweave turned to Detteras. "Rundle, what of you?"

Detteras rolled up his eyes. "I am a rational man; I can't have blind faith—in you, in Gersen or in anyone else. Gersen has made a case and, astonishing as it is, the

150

facts seem to bear him out. Can you demonstrate to the contrary?"

Warweave considered. "I believe so." He strolled to the shelf below which Suthiro had installed the switch. The inhalator he had worn outside dangled from his hand. "Yes," said Warweave, "I believe I can make a convincing case for myself." He pressed the inhalator to his face, touched the switch. At the forward console the air-pollution alarm sounded, a raucous loud clanging.

"If you turn back the switch," Gersen called out, "the noise will stop."

Warweave numbly reached blow the shelf, reversed the switch.

Gersen turned to Kelle and Detteras. "Warweave is as surprised as you. He thought that the switch controlled the gas reservoirs which you will find under the settees; hence his use of the inhalator. I emptied the tanks and changed the leads of the switch."

Kelle looked under the settee, brought forth the canister. He looked at Warweave. "Well, Gyle?"

Warweave tossed aside the inhalator, turned his back in disgust.

Detteras suddenly roared, "Warweave! Let's have the truth!"

Warweave spoke over his shoulder. "You've heard the truth. From Gersen."

"You are—Malagate?" said Detteras in a hushed voice.

"Yes." Warweave wheeled about, drew himself up to his full height. His black eyes glared back and forth. "And I am a Star King, superior to men!"

"A man has defeated you," said Kelle.

Warweave's eyes burnt even brighter. He turned to consider Gersen. "I am curious. Ever since your encounter with Lugo Teehalt you have sought Malagate. Why?"

"Malagate is one of the Demon Princes. I hope to destroy each of them."

"So what is your intention in regard to me?"

"I plan to kill you."

Warweave thought for a moment. "You are an ambitious man," he said in a neutral voice. "There are not many like you."

"There were not many survivors of the raid on Mount Pleasant. My grandfather was one. I was another."

"Indeed," said Warweave. "The Mount Pleasant raid. So long ago."

"This is a peculiar voyage," said Kelle, whose attitude had become one of wry detachment. "At least we have achieved our ostensible purpose. The planet exists; it is as Mr. Gersen described it, and the money in escrow becomes his property."

"Not until we return to Alphanor," growled Detteras.

Gersen spoke to Warweave. "You have taken great pains to secure this world for yourself. I wonder why."

Warweave shrugged noncommittally.

"A man might want to live here, or build himself a palace," suggested Gersen. "A Star King wants none of these things."

Warweave said presently, "You make a common mistake. Men are after all quite parochial. You forget that individual differences exist among folk other than yourselves. Some perhaps are denied the freedom of their own worlds. They become 'renegade': neither man nor their own kind. The folk of Ghnarumen—" he easily used the name which sounded like a cough—" are quite as orderly as the most law-abiding folk of the Oikumene. In short, the career of Malagate is not one which the folk of Ghnarumen would care to emulate. They may be right, they may be wrong. It is my prerogative to organize my own style of life. As you know, the Star Kings are strongly competitive. This world, to men, is beautiful. I find it pleasant enough. I plan to bring here folk of my race, to nurture them on a world more beautiful than Earth, to father a world and a people superior to both men and the people of Ghnarumen. This was my hope, which you will not understand, for there can be no such understanding between your race and mine."

Detteras said between clenched teeth, "But you took advantage of our liberality to dishonor us. If Gersen doesn't kill you, I will."

"Neither of you will kill Malagate the Star King." Two steps took him to the exit port. Detteras lunged after him, frustrating Gersen's attempt to use his projac. Warweave turned, lashed out with his foot, kicked Detteras in the stomach, jumped to the ground, ran off down the slope.

Gersen stepped to the exit port, aimed, sent a bolt of energy unsuccessfully after the bounding figure. He descended the ladder, gave chase. Warweave reached the meadow, hesitated at the edge of the river, looked back at Gersen, continued down the valley. Gersen kept to the upper slopes where the ground was hard, and began to gain on Warweave, who had come to a marshy area. Warweave once more went to the riverbank, hesitated. If he plunged in, before he gained the opposite shore Gersen would be upon him. He looked back over his shoulder, and his face was no longer that of a man; Gersen wondered how he could have been fooled even for an instant. Warweave turned, uttered a cry in a slurred guttural language, went to his knees, disappeared.

Gersen, reaching the spot, found a hole in the riverbank almost two feet across. He bent, peered in, but saw nothing. Detteras and Kelle ran up, panting. "Where is he?"

Gersen pointed to the burrow. "According to Lugo Teehalt, large white grubs live under the marsh."

"Hmf," said Detteras. "His ancestors evolved in the swamps, in just such holes. He probably couldn't want a better haven."

Kelle said dubiously, "He'll have to come out—to eat, to drink."

"I'm not so sure. The Star Kings dislike human food; men find the Star King diet equally repellent. We cultivate plants and domesticate animals; they do similarly for worms and insects, such things as that. Warweave should do quite well on what he finds underground."

Gersen looked up the valley where Hildemar Dasce had fled. "I've lost them both. I was willing to sacrifice Dasce to get Malagate—but both...."

The three stood on the riverbank. A breeze rippled the surface of the water, moved the branches of the great dark trees which grew at the base of the hills. A tribe of dryads wandering along the opposite shore turned their purple-green eye smudges on the men.

Gersen said, "Perhaps it's just as bad, leaving them together on this planet, as killing them."

"Worse," said Detteras devoutly. "Worse by far."

They returned slowly to the ship. Pallis Atwrode, sitting on the turf, rose to her feet as Gersen approached. She seemed not so much oblivious to the events of the past few minutes as uninterested, unconcerned. She came over to him, took his arm, smiled up into his face. Her own face was once again vital and fresh.

"Kirth, I like it here, don't you?"

"Yes, Pallis, very much."

"Imagine!" said Pallis in a hushed voice. "A pretty house up there on the hill. Old Sir Morton Hodenfroe had a beautiful house up along Blackstone Edge. Wouldn't that be nice, Kirth? I wonder. I wonder...."

"First we must return to Alphanor, Pallis. Then we'll talk about coming back."

"Very well, Kirth." She hesitated, then put her arms up to his shoulders, wistfully searched his face. "Do you still ... are you still—interested in me? After what happened?"

"Of course." Gersen's eyes felt moist. "What fault was it of yours?"

"None. . . . But at home, in Lantango, men are very jealous."

Gersen could think of nothing to say. He kissed her forehead, patted her shoulders.

Detteras said gruffly, "Well, Gersen, you've made use of Kelle and myself in a most cavalier fashion. I can't say that I enjoyed it, but I can't bring myself to resent it, either."

Robin Rampold approached slowly, keeping to the shadow of the ship. "Hildemar ran away," he said mournfully. "Now he will make over the mountains to town and I will never see him again."

"He can make over the mountains," said Gersen, "but he won't find any towns."

"I have been watching up along the hillside, and through the forest," said Rampold. "I think he is somewhere nearby."

"Very likely," said Gersen.

"It is distressing," said Rampold. "It is enough to sadden a man."

Gersen laughed. "You would prefer to be back in the cage?"

"No, of course not. But then I had my dreams. Of what I would do when I won free. Seventeen years of hopes and dreams. But now I am free and Hildemar is beyond my reach." He moved disconsolately away.

After a pause Kelle said, "As a scientist I find this planet a place of fascination. As a man I find it entrancing. As Kagge Kelle, erstwhile colleague of Gyle Warweave—I find it extremely depressing. I am prepared to leave at any time."

"Yes," said Detteras in a gruff voice. "Why not?"

Gersen looked up the valley to where Hildemar Dasce, wearing only soiled white pantaloons, lurked in the forest like a raging, desperate beast. He looked down the valley, far down over the hazy plain, then back to the swampy meadow, under which crawled Malagate the Woe. He looked down into the face of Pallis Atwrode.

She took a deep breath. "I can't believe this is real."

"It's real. But it's also a dream."

"All the rest seems a dream too. A terrible dream."

"It's over now. As if it had never happened."

"I've been. . . ." She hesitated, frowned. "I don't remember too much."

"Just as well."

"Pallis pointed across the meadow. "Look, Kirth; what are those beautiful creatures?"

"Dryads."

"What are they doing out there?"

"I don't know. Looking for something to eat, I suppose. Lugo Teehalt says they suck up nourishment from big grubs which burrow under the meadow. Or perhaps they lay eggs in the soil."

The dryads, wandering up the shore, flourished their gorgeous fronds, swaying slowly like branches in the wind. On the swamp they moved more slowly, a step at a time. One of them stopped, stood stock still. Under its foot showed a glint of white, as the concealed proboscis plunged down into the soft ground. A few seconds passed. The ground heaved, erupted: the dryad toppled over backward. Up from a crater staggered Warweave, the proboscis still thrust through his back. His face was stained with dirt, his eyes stared from his head; from his mouth issued a series of appalling cries. He shook himself, fell to his knees, rolled over, disengaged himself from the fluttering dryad, jumped erect, ran crazily up the hillside. His steps flagged. He fell to his knees, clutched at the ground, kicked and lay still.

* * * * * * *

Gyle Warweave was buried on the hillside. The group returned to the ship. Robin Rampold now diffidently approached Gersen. "I have made up my mind to stay here."

In one part of his brain Gersen was shocked and astonished. In another part there was only confirmation of a previous expectation. "So," said Gersen heavily, "you expect to live on this planet with Hildemar Dasce."

"Yes."

"Do you know what will happen? He will make you his slave. Or he will kill you for the food which I shall be bound to leave you."

Rampold's face was bleak and drawn. "It may be as you say. But I cannot leave Hildemar Dasce."

"Think," said Gersen. "You will be here alone. He will be more savage than ever before."

"I hope that you will leave me certain articles: a weapon, a shovel, a few tools to build a shelter, some food."

"And what will you do when the food runs out?"

"I will look for natural food: seeds, fish, nuts, roots. These may be poisonous, but I will test them carefully. And what else is left for me?"

Gersen shook his head. "Far better that you return with us to Alphanor. Hildemar Dasce will take revenge on you."

Robin Rampold said, "It is a chance I must take."

"As you wish."

The ship lifted from the meadow, leaving Rampold standing beside his meager stack of supplies.

The horizons spread out, the planet became a green and blue ball and fell astern. Gersen turned to Kelle and Detteras. "Well, gentlemen, you have visited Teehalt's planet."

"Yes," said Kelle tonelessly. "By a roundabout method you have fulfilled the terms of your agreement; the money is yours."

Gersen shook his head. "I don't want the money. I suggest that we keep the existence of this planet secret, to preserve it from what could only be desecration."

"Very well," said Kelle. "I'm agreed."

"I agree," said Detteras, "provided that I may return another time, under more relaxing circumstances."

"One further condition," said Gersen. "A third of the funds in escrow were deposited by Attel Malagate. I suggest that they be transferred to Miss Atwrode's account, as some measure of compensation for the wrongs done her at Malagate's orders."

Neither Kelle nor Detteras made objection. Pallis protested half-heartedly, then acquiesced, and presently became very cheerful.

And astern the yellow-white star became one with the multitude, and presently vanished.

* * * * * * *

A year later Kirth Gersen returned alone to Teehalt's planet in his old Model 9B spaceboat.

Hanging in space, he examined the valley by macroscope, but discovered no signs of life. There was now a projac on the planet and it might well be in the hands of Hildemar Dasce. He waited till nightfall and landed the boat on a shelf in the mountains above the river valley.

The long quiet night came to an end. At dawn Gersen

started down the valley, keeping always to the shelter of the trees.

From far off he heard the sound of an ax. With great care he approached the sound.

On the edge of the forest Robin Rampold chopped at a fallen tree. Gersen stealthily moved closer. Rampold's face had filled out. He looked bronzed and strong and fit. Gersen called his name. Rampold looked up, startled, searched the dark shadows. "Who is there?"

"Kirth Gersen."

"Come forth, come forth. No need to steal up so furtively."

Gersen moved to the edge of the forest, looked carefully all around. "I feared I might find Hildemar Dasce."

"Ah," said Rampold. "No need to worry about Hildemar."

"He is dead?"

"No. He is quite alive, in a little pen I built for him. With your permission, I will not take you to see him, as the pen is in a private spot, well hidden from any who might visit the planet."

"I see," said Gersen. "You defeated Dasce, then."

"Of course. Did you ever doubt it? I have much more resource than he. I dug a pit during the night, built a deadfall. In the morning Hildemar Dasce swaggered forth, hoping to confiscate my stores. He fell into it, and I took him captive. Already he has become a changed man." He looked closely into Gersen's face. "You do not approve?"

Gersen shrugged. "I came to take you back to the Oikumene."

"No," said Rampold. "Never fear for me. I will live out my days here, with Hildemar Dasce. It is a beautiful planet. I have found sufficient food to maintain us, and daily I demonstrate to Hildemar Dasce the tricks and conceits he taught me long ago."

They wandered down the valley to the previous landing place. "The life cycle here is strange," said Rampold. "Each form changes into another, endlessly. Only the trees are permanent."

"So I learned from the man who first found the planet."

"Come, I'll show you Warweave's grave." Rampold led the way up the slope, to a copse of slender white-timbered trees. To the side grew a seedling, rather different from the rest. The trunk was veined with purple, the leaves were dark-green and leathery. Rampold pointed. "There rests Gyle Warweave."

Gersen looked for a moment, then turned away. He gazed up and down the valley. It was as beautiful and placid and quiet as before. "Well, then," said Gersen, "I will once more depart. I may never return. Are you sure you wish to stay?"

"Absolutely." Rampold looked up at the sun. "But I am late. Hildemar will be expecting me. A pity to disappoint him. I will bid you farewell now." He bowed and departed, crossing the valley and disappearing into the forest.

Gersen once more looked up and down the valley. This world was no longer innocent; it had known evil. A sense of tarnish lay across the panorama. Gersen sighed, turned, stood looking down at Warweave's grave. He bent, seized the seedling, pulled it from the soil, broke it, cast it aside. Then he turned and walked up the valley toward his spaceboat.

You will also enjoy these other outstanding

BERKLEY

SCIENCE FICTION TITLES

(please turn page)

F743	SHIELD	Poul Anderson
F760	IN DEEP	Damon Knight
F780	A TRACE OF MEMORY	Keith Laumer
F799	BUDRYS' INFERNO	Algis Budrys
F812	AWAY AND BEYOND	A. E. van Vogt
F823	PASSPORT TO ETERNITY	J. G. Ballard
F835	STRANGERS IN THE UNIVERSE	Clifford D. Simak
F851	SCIENCE FICTION OMNIBUS	Groff Conklin, ed.
F862	THE MILE-LONG SPACESHIP	Kate Wilhelm
F875	THE ASTOUNDING SCIENCE FICTION ANTHOLOGY	John W. Campbell, Jr., ed.
F883	LAMBDA I AND OTHER STORIES	John Carnell, ed.
F893	DESTINATION: UNIVERSE!	A. E. van Vogt

These books are available at your local newsstand or

ORDER ANY FOUR FOR $2.00
POSTAGE FREE!

On single copy orders send 50¢ plus 10¢ for postage and handling to BERKLEY PUBLISHING CORPORATION, 15 East 26th Street, New York, N. Y. 10010